IREMONGER

BOOK 2

FOULSHAM

written and illustrated by
E D W A R D   C A R E Y

The Overlook Press
New York, NY

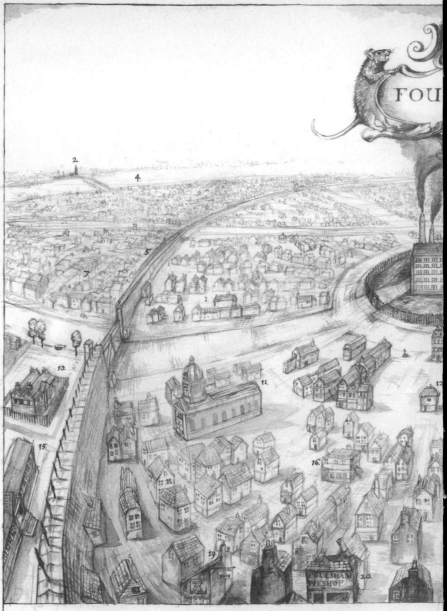

FOU

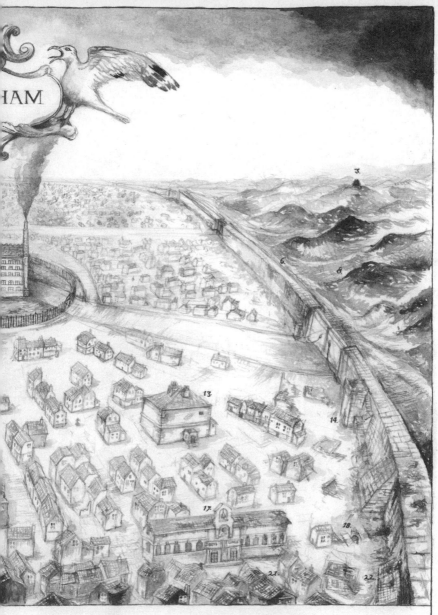

This edition first published in paperback in the United States in 2015 by
The Overlook Press, Peter Mayer Publishers, Inc.
141 Wooster Street
New York, NY 10012
www.overlookpress.com

For bulk and special sales, please contact sales@overlookny.com,
or write us at the above address.

Library of Congress Cataloging-in-Publication Data
Carey, Edward, 1970- author, illustrator.
Foulsham / written and illustrated by Edward Carey.
pages cm. -- (Iremonger ; book 2)
Originally published in the United Kingdom by Hot Key Books in 2014.
ISBN 978-1-4683-0954-6 (hardback)
[1. Fantasy. 2. Refuse and refuse disposal--Fiction.] I. Title.
PZ7.C21226Fo 2015
[Fic]--dc23
                    2015011874

Printed in the United States of America
ISBN 978-1-4683-1178-5
1 3 5 7 9 8 6 4 2

For Gus

Part One

Foulsham Streets

James Henry Hayward
and his Governess Ada Cruickshanks

I

OBSERVATIONS FROM A NURSERY

The narrative of James Henry Hayward,
property of Bayleaf House Factory,
Forlichingham, London

They told me I was the only child in the whole great building, but I wasn't. I knew I wasn't. I heard them sometimes, the other children. I heard them calling out somewhere down below.

I lived in a mean room with my governess. Ada Cruickshanks was her name. 'Miss Cruickshanks' I had to call her. She gave me physic very often from a tablespoon, it had a strange enough smell to it, but it felt very warming inside, as if it took away winter. I was given sweet things to eat, I had pound cake and tea cake, I had Forlichingham Pie too, which, in truth, was not my absolute favourite, the top of it being somewhat burnt according to tradition and the insides rather a swill bucket of left-overs all covered over in sweet black treacle to disguise the taste. Miss Cruickshanks said that I must eat it all up, she would be cross with me if I didn't. So then I ate it.

She would tell me odd stories, Miss Cruickshanks would, not from a book, but from her head, she should sit by me and looking sternly she should begin, 'Now listen, child, this is the truth of it.

'There are two types of people, those that know about objects and those others that don't. And I'm one of the former grouping, and so I can tell you. I can tell you that once there was a place where the objects didn't do what they were told. In that place, I shan't tell you its name, I shall not be so bold, in that place people had got so thick and muddled about with things that things may have appeared a human and a human likewise be struck down a thing. In that place you must have been very careful with whatever you picked up, for you may have thought it just a common teacup when in fact it was someone called Frederick Smith who'd been turned into a cup. And amongst that place there were high lords of things, terrible bailiffs, who may turn a person into a thing without ever much caring about it. What do you think about that?'

'I hardly know what to think about it, Miss Cruickshanks.'

'Well then, consider it until you do.'

Often she would ask me, 'Do you still have it? Show me now! Show me!' I would take the golden half sovereign out of my pocket and show it her. I always had to keep this particular coin with me, my own sov it was. What a fuss they made over it. If I took it out in public the people around in the big old place gasped at it, and then Miss Cruickshanks shrieked,

'Put it away! Put it out of sight! It isn't safe! It's not safe!

You never know who's looking!'

Once in a while I would be summoned out of the nursery rooms to visit an old man. I should be sent into his grand room with all its shelves, and he would let me look at the things on the shelves, but not to touch them. Such odd things there were, some of it just rubbish, bits of old pipes, or a roof tile, an old tin mug, but others that shone and were silver or golden. I did not know why he kept them all. I supposed they were his special collection. I thought I would like to have a collection of my own someday.

The first business I had always to do when visiting the old man was show him my sov. I brought it to him and I dropped it into his large wrinkled hands. He studied it and turned it over and over. He was very content to do this for some time. At last he would return it to me and watch me place it deep in my pocket.

'I am pleased with you, young James Henry. You do good work.'

'Thank you, sir. I should very much like to work, sir, if it is with you.'

'Owner Umbitt is a very busy man,' said Miss Cruickshanks.

'You must never spend that sovereign, James Henry,' the old man told me.

'I know, sir. I do know that,' I said, because he reminded me of it each visit.

'Say it to me, James Henry.' Very serious now.

'I am never to spend my sovereign.'

Where ever should I spend it anyway? There was certainly

nowhere in the factory, and I was never allowed out into town. How they went on about it, over and over. Do not spend. Never to spend.

'Good child,' the old man said. 'Mrs Groom shall bake you something. She is a most excellent cook, the best in all Forlichingham. How lucky we are that she sends us food here to Bayleaf House.' And then I should have to make a small bow to him and be taken back to the nursery.

Bayleaf House, my home, was the tallest, grandest place in all the whole borough. Built like a great weight it was, like an anchor. It was a certain place. It wasn't going anywhere. You might sleep easy in such a place, knowing that when you woke up in the morning Bayleaf should still be standing. Yes, what a place it was! How fortunate I was with all the good things to eat!

Actually, it was them that told me how fortunate I was to be there, over and over. I was not sure I felt very fortunate. Bayleaf House was some sort of factory, though what exactly it made I could not tell. It was very hot in places. There were ovens and chimneys that poured out smoke. They smothered the rest of the borough with soot.

There were pipes all over the house, great metal pipes that snaked over the ceilings that columned the walls, sometimes a hundred thick and more. They got everywhere those pipes. I doubt there was a single room in the whole place that didn't have pipes inside it. Some of these pipes were cold to touch, very cold, and some were awful hot and could scald you.

There were so many rooms where I was not permitted.

You're not to go in there, boy, do you hear? That place is not for you. Keep clear of the second floor, of the third. Where are the bells sounding from? I would ask. That is none of your business, they would say. What do all the whistles mean that blow day and night, I wondered. That need not concern you, they replied.

So, all in all, it must be said, I knew very little of Bayleaf House. Sometimes I heard the house about its business. I might hear people calling out, calls that sounded as if someone not very far off was hurting. They were children's voices, I'd swear on it. When I heard the calling I got unsettled. And then Ada Cruickshanks picked up a hammer and banged it upon the pipes. Then, after a moment, the calling would often stop.

'I heard them, Miss Cruickshanks! I heard children!'

'You did not.'

'I know I did.'

'You know nothing.'

Well, and that was true enough.

I knew that my name was James Henry Hayward, that I lived in the London borough of Filching, just by the great waste heaps. I knew that I was born here, in Filching. I have the place in my blood. But it was Miss Cruickshanks who told me all that, it was not something that I remembered. She called me gutter-born.

I tried so hard to remember my family but I could not. What did my mother look like, my father? Did I have any brothers or sisters? Why was I stuck inside with her and not out there with them? How did I come to be in this great house? Why did I live in a factory at all?

'Might I go out?' I asked her, 'Are my family still living there? I can't really remember them. May I go and see them?'

'No, no!' she snapped, 'Dirty! You'll get filthy out there. You'd get yourself lost, out in Forlichingham. It's not safe, there are terrible people, thieves and murderers. Come away from the window, how many times must I tell you!' Then she'd turn on me. 'Do you still have it? Show me! Show me!' And I'd show her the coin.

It was all smallholdings, Filching was. I saw it from the window, little places a bit derelict here and there, smashed windows, holes in roofs, buildings propped up, jerry-built, that sort of thing.

I saw the heap wall that protected Filching from all the mass of dirtheaps, and on the other side of the dirty town was the other wall. The wall that kept Filching from London itself. That wall was taller than the heap wall and more recently built. It had spikes on the top it did, and beyond it was London, true London, so near to us, so close but so far away because that London we should never enter. London was an impossible place to us people of Filching. No Trespassing.

Beneath my window, just beyond the factory railing, was the very nearest part of Filching to Bayleaf House. It was a tall white building, people kept running in and out of it. I liked to watch it. When I looked out from the windows and saw the crooked town I knew I loved it. I knew that I longed to get out into it, to be in those winding dark streets. Somewhere out there was my family.

I got terror headaches, and when I got them, when my poor old top smarted from all my thinking, then Miss Cruickshanks brought me the physic on the tablespoon. You felt so warm inside after eating it and the headache went right away and it all rather fogged over, but in a very nice way. All in all, I'd say, it was always foggy for me. I knew so little, so much was kept from me, that I lived in a smog. And on top of that, or confirming it really, was Miss Cruickshanks who wore a black bonnet that had a veil to it, so that I could not see her face properly. It was kept from me. I saw just hints of it, shadows under the veil. I never saw it properly. I could not say what she actually looked like.

But even after taking the physic, I could not stop thinking about my people out there in Filching.

'Do you know where my parents are?' I asked her.

'There are greater matters at stake.'

'I would like to visit them. If they are there, beyond the gates.'

'Well, you can't, boy. You mustn't.'

'Why may I not?'

'Questions! Questions! Nothing but questions. Your questions peck at me like beaks, they scratch into me and send me into a fury. Let me tell you then, that which others would spare you: the place is dangerous and rickety, full of disease and cruelty. They don't say Filching any more, the common people, they call it Foulsham these days, because it is a stinking, quagmire of a place, thick with pestilence.

'A man they call the Tailor hides in the alleys out there and murders people – and the people out there are of such little worth that no one makes much of a fuss about it. Step out,

James Henry Hayward, and you would not last a minute. You cannot be safe out there. The very air is pestilential. Step out and die, step out and crumble, step out and shatter.'

'But there are people out there. I have seen them in the dark streets.'

'Rat people, roach people. Ill people, dying people.'

I think it must have been the mention of rat people that jogged my memory, for I suddenly found myself remembering something I hadn't before. I remembered a house, I recalled a room in a house with a dirt floor. There was a cupboard there, a door to it. I remembered opening the cupboard door, there was a little girl inside putting her finger to her lips to shush me. I remembered that! I remembered something! I couldn't tell who she was, at first, or where I'd dreamt up such a thing. But I liked the thought of it. I kept trying to picture that face, but each time when I went back to it in my mind, when I opened the cupboard again in my thoughts the girl was not there, and in her place was a rat.

The night after I'd remembered the girl in the cupboard, I heard Miss Cruickshanks muttering away in her side room. I wondered what she was muttering about so furiously. She'd already twice come tiptoeing in to see if I was asleep and to make sure I had the half sovereign beneath my pillow, and so I think she must have felt sure I was finally sleeping. I wasn't though and I quietly, so quietly, got out of my bed, and so, so silently moved across the floor and then looked into her room and there she was, sitting on the side of her bed with a looking glass in her hands, and I saw her lift up her veil. And then I saw her face. Oh, the shock of it!

There was a great crack down the centre of it! A great rent running down the middle! Like she was a bit of pottery and not a person at all!

'Evil child!' she screamed, turning round.

'I'm so sorry, Miss Cruickshanks. I didn't mean to.'

'Horrible little thief!'

'Does it hurt, Miss Cruickshanks? Your cut I mean? I am very sorry for it, I did not know you were hurt. Excuse me, miss.'

'I hate you!'

'Yes, Miss Cruickshanks.'

'I hope you rot!'

'Yes, Miss Cruickshanks.'

'Take your medicine. Now.'

'Yes, Miss Cruickshanks.'

'We are stuck with each other, child.'

'Yes, Miss Cruickshanks.'

'Go to bed!'

Seeing her wounded face made me feel different about her. Poor old Cruickshanks, I resolved to think of her more kindly. Cruickshanks was a person and a woman to boot, with all those woman things around her, all those bits and pieces signifying a female. I didn't like to credit the thought.

I preferred not to take my physic so much afterwards, I didn't want to be so fogged over. I began to pretend to take it. I'd slip it in my pocket. I'd spit it out when I had a chance. All that thick whiteness went away and I could focus again. My head hurt perpetually, but I remembered more. I remembered the girl in a cupboard, I saw her better.

She was hiding there; it was her secret place. She kept her rag doll in there. I began to wonder if the girl was my sister. I began to be certain she was. And with that certainty I remembered more than a cupboard. I saw a whole room and people in it. An old woman coughing, a younger woman and man. There was a boy then as well, all busy about some activity. I could not tell what it was at first. Then forcing myself, I began to see more. I could look over their shoulders. They were making small cages. Cages, cages for what? I looked up, there were cages, any amount of them, hanging from the ceilings, there were birds in some of these cages, scruffy seagulls and dusty pigeons.

And there were other cages on the ground. The ones on the ground had a sort of shutter to them on a spring. Then I knew it! Then I had it! Traps! Rat traps, they were rat traps. That's what they were, they were ratters, these people. They were champion rat catchers. How my heart raced at that. Yes, yes I knew them. I knew them and I loved them. They were my family. My family were great ratters of Filching!

There was my father, strong and burly, scratches all over his hands and face, what a champion rat catcher he was! There, my mother, scratched over a good deal too, fierce and fond. Yes I know you, Mother. My brother, learning to make a mouse trap. My sister and her rag doll, not a rag doll, a rag rat she had, a rat in a dress. My grandmother in the corner, fixing traps, two of her fingers missing from her early hunting days. What stories she used to tell us of those, of grandfather and wharf rats! And there was my grandfather, bent over, but grinning. Oh my family, my family. They all came flooding back to me.

14

How I loved to be there with all of them.

There was more I saw, there was me amongst them all, going out with father in his leathers to hunt, to lay down the traps. And there was the outside of the house, a one-storey place, fairly rickety, but with a shop sign flapping merrily in the wind, HAYWARD RAT CATCHERS FULLY LICENSED BY APPOINTMENT TO TUNCRID IREMONGER, GENT. Yes, home, what a home it was! And there pasted on the walls, the bill stickers, RATS FOR SALE, and MOUSETRAPS, FLYPAPERS, GULLTRAPS, GULL MEAT, RAT RACKS, TAXIDERMY, WE ARTICULATE!, FEATHERS BY THE SACK, SKINS! What a home it was, what a place! That was it, the House of Rats, that was my place, that was where my people were. I had to find it.

The House of Rats.

Home.

That was the start of it. From then on I needed to learn more. Miss Cruckshanks kept a diary. I had seen her at it often enough, but I never should have thought to look at it, not until after I stopped taking the physic. She went out every day, locking the door behind her, to give her report to the old man. And so I took out her diary, and I read there all the thoughts of my governess, and those words brought even more confusion into my head,

I split. I crack. I am coming apart. Every day a little more.

One day, one day soon, I shall be in pieces.

Do not let me shatter, keep me in one part. I want, I so want to stay whole. But they say that I shall not. They say it is hopeless for me. They say I have the fever and that in time I shall fall to pieces. Shall it be tomorrow, I ask. Shall I be broken tomorrow? They tell me perhaps, though it is not likely. There is some time yet. Probably.

A little further on I read,

Sometimes, in the night, if I am very quiet, I can hear myself splitting. My skin when I tap it lightly makes a noise. It should not make a noise. I should not sound like porcelain. I look at cups and saucers, at plates and bowls with disgust now. Is that what I am? A china thing?

I heard her outside then, and was quick to put the diary back. The next chance I had I read further and longer.

My parents were from Italy, from Napoli, they were cheap performers, they sang and danced a little. They had a dog who did tricks, and they had me too. The theatre they were working in, The Heaving Heap in Filching, always a braced-up building, never a steady place, one day collapsed. So many died that night, the night that I was left alone. I hadn't been performing with them. I was outside the theatre with the sandwich board trying to get people to buy tickets. I was ten then already and so able enough to stand up on my own. My family name was Crenzini and that came with much prejudice; it showed us up as foreign and alien, so I called myself Cruickshanks after Mama and Papa died because I thought it sounded hard and respectful and English. And no nonsense. The Ada I have always had with me.

I found work as an assistant to a Filching schoolmistress. I was very strict. I worked so hard not to sound Italian, and I must have had some of my parents' theatrics because people found me clipped and upright and quite believable. "You're quite a woman already, Ada, aren't you? I suppose you were born grown up," she told me. I learnt from the mistress and soon could teach English myself. A great bully she was, Mistress Winthrop, but so thick with gin that she was ever more gin than human, more bottle than body. It may as well have been that transparent perfumed stuff swilling through her veins and not blood at all. I did more and more of the teaching.

She could not be blamed perhaps; she had been brought low. Her husband who had been the schoolmaster was nowhere to be found. He'd upped and left, and the mistress remembered him often while polishing a small rubber truncheon that she never let out of her sight. This truncheon, it now seems to me, actually was her husband only in his changed state.

And then one morning several of the children had

17

gone missing, one whole form – my form. There was no one there, but such a chaos of objects that I had never known before: a brass cymbal, a milk jug, a horse whip, a fish hook. I said I did not know how such a thing had happened. I was called forth and given something to eat by a very kind-seeming man and that is the last I remember.

That much, and no more. It is enough. I wish to go forwards not back again. I wish to remain Ada. To make her more solid than she has ever been before, it was a tenuous hold I had on life when I worked in Filching schools. I would like to live. This is the testament of Ada Cruickshanks. I am Ada Cruickshanks.

The last time I read from the diary, I found this passage:

Each person in the Iremonger circle must keep his thing to him, his birth object. You shall not last long without it; the disease shall come upon you. But I have lost mine. It was a clay button I am told, but is lost, lost for ever. And to think I must spend my precious time with the child who takes his birth object, that shining sovereign, and polishes it and plays with it not knowing how he thus mocks me. How he clings to it, and how they make such a fuss of it, for, they tell me so, there's a person trapped inside that half sovereign, an important person.

The person that is trapped in the sovereign has power over objects enough to rival Umbitt. I have been told

*that he, when he was a person, had somehow – because
he had fallen in love with a common servant – sent all
the objects into a turmoil. And so, if he could do that,
if he could upset all because he had fallen in love –
because in those moments he had such feelings – then
what else might he be capable of? He was dangerous,
I am told, and a wonder. For now, he must be kept as
a sovereign where he may do no harm. He may be
terminated. Umbitt might murder him, it has not been
decided yet. They debate whether to ever let him out
again. How could I tell the child that they are waiting
to decide if he should live or no?*

*Sometimes I look at the sovereign and I wonder if it
were a person again could it help me? And what then,
I wonder, should happen to the poor dumb child? How
I should dearly like to warn him, but what good should
that do?*

*We are bound by some dark love. We are its opposite,
its reverse. We suppress it, James Henry Hayward and
I. We have snuffed it out, that forbidden loving. It is not
our choice perhaps. And yet it is so.*

*And yet, and yet, despite their efforts, I think it is
already coming undone.*

*They who live here around us see it, that old passion
finding itself again. The truth of it is in my cracking. I
am breaking up.*

I could not fully understand the passage, though there was
surely that within the diary which terrified me. I resolved that

the first ever opportunity I had I should be out of there and run into the Foulsham streets. I should search for my family. I should find my people. All my thoughts were on my escape, on my freedom, all I could think of was breathing air beyond Bayleaf House. I should have to take their precious coin with me, for a half sov was a deal of money and I should need to have that about me.

I waited. I tucked myself up in my bed and waited. I waited for them to make a mistake. I lay blank before them, feeble and compliant, but my head inside me raged and raced!

It happened right enough one morning. One early morning before the sun was quite up, when there were less people about, before the ritual of medicine and prodding and coin lifting.

The mornings should generally begin with Miss Cruickshanks shaking herself up from the room beyond and then coming to talk at me through her veil. But she never came, not that morning.

I crept out then. I looked over. Still nothing. I slipped out of bed. I crept over to the door, even braved myself to look beyond into her room. And she was not there. No Cruickshanks not for love nor money. She had been there though, sure enough. Her bed was unmade. Very unlike Cruickshanks that was. Then I saw that there was something in her bed, something other than sheets and blankets, something in the middle where the Cruickshanks body should generally be. I couldn't see it very clearly. It was still dark, but a grey light was beginning to come. I got closer and even put my hand out towards it. It was a box of matches, an ordinary box of matches. How did that get in there? Perhaps it had fallen from her bedside table, for there was a candle there in a brass holder, and yet there was a lucifer beside it. Bringing the box from the bed up to my face I saw that it said SEALED FOR YOUR CONVENIENCE.

I needed more light, some light to help me, so I tore it off and straight away took out one of the matches. Struck it, it didn't light. Struck it again, and what a sizzling strange flame came off it! A weak, sad flame, barely enough to light the candle before it fizzled out.

'Miss Cruickshanks? Miss Cruickshanks?' I whispered.

Not a sign of her, her clothes were there though. Her black dress laid out on the chair ready for her to put on, lying there like a deflated Cruickshanks, and there too was her terrible bonnet with its black veil, and all them outer things of Cruickshanks, waiting in the place. Waiting for Cruickshanks to tug them on to herself to cover herself up. Had she gone out in her nightdress?

And that was what gave me the idea.

Could I?

Could I do it?

The sun was still not all awake. It was dark yet. It was better to do it now. I'd have a greater chance if I was about it straight away. Yes! I would do it! I would dress myself up in Cruickshanks' clothes. I'd be Cruickshanks with the veil over me and that way I'd get me out of there. What a plan! What recklessness! To wear all them women's things! It wasn't to be countenanced. Well then, show me another plan. Give me another way. There was no other way. It was only this or nothing else.

So then.

I put my own clothes on underneath. I tugged Cruickshanks' dress over me. It was tight, she was such a lean one. It felt horrible, but I must do it. On, on! Hurry yourself James Henry Hayward. You're more James Henry Hayward today than you have been in many a day, whether you wear women's clothes or no. I tied the bonnet on, I pulled the veil down. I picked up Cruickshanks' looking glass and looked through it, well there was a shadowy face beneath the veil, one that was not like Cruickshanks, but maybe, I thought, maybe in the half-light: get you going!

I was in her black lace-up boots, which gave me some extra height. I was all ready by the door. I had the key, it was around her belt. I had the key in the door, ready to head out. Wait though! Wait up! I went back to my bed, lifted my pillow, took up my half sovereign. There then! I plopped it fair and square in Cruickshanks' pocket and then, only then did I turn the key in the lock and open the door.

There was a guard there. I was expecting that, right beside me, upon a high stool. He stood up when he saw me, drowsy he was, napping I think. He stirred himself.

'Sorry, Miss Cruickshanks,' he said, 'I was awake, honest mum.'

I made a Cruickshanks-like snort. That was the advantage of pretending to be such a strict one that grunted so: I did not have to speak.

'Going out are you, Miss Cruickshanks?' the guard asked.

I locked the nursery door, put the key back on the belt.

'Not like you is it, Miss Cruickshanks? Not like you to go

out of a morning. Everything all right is it?'

I gave a single brief nod.

'Anything I could do?' he asked.

A very brief shake of my bonneted head, and I threw in a grunt for good measure, to tell the guard he should not presume. I went down then. I clacked down the stairs in that horrible bootwear. I wobbled a bit I suppose, and nearly fell upon my face.

'Are you sure you are quite all right, Miss Cruickshanks?' the guard called down.

My answer was a furious, 'Sssssshhh!'

I had to hope that had done it. I turned the corner then, the nursery was out of sight. I went down, down Bayleaf House, even to the ground floor. No one had stopped me yet. Every trembling footstep took me closer to victory. I was soon enough in one of the offices below, people readying for the day's business, all the desks there, all the pipes and people running this way and that. I passed through them.

Sometimes people stopped and bowed to me, but on I went, on and on. There was a sudden loud shriek which nearly set me screaming: I've been found out, I've been discovered. But it was only the noise of the black steam-engine coming in from the heaps. The old man would be arriving now, coming up into Bayleaf House for the day's business. In former days I should be made happy by that sound, comforted by it. But not now, not any longer. I walked on, people passed by. Keep going, I told myself, keep going, with purpose. And there, there right ahead was the main door, the entrance way out of this place, and I walked to it, didn't I, and the doorman opened it, didn't he. And I walked on, just me doing that, no one else, I walked to the gate, right up to the gate. I spoke then, clearing my voice,

'Let me out,' I said, as strict as I may.

'You want to go out, miss, into Foulsham?'

'Out,' I said.

'Yes, miss, if you're certain.'

I nodded, and the gate was opened, and I was through. I hurried on down the street, I was outside! Passed the tall white building that I had often watched from the nursery window. I could see the other side of it then, see more of it than I ever managed before. There was writing on the front wall of it, MRS WHITING'S CLEAN HOUSE it said. ROOMS TO LET. There was an odd little man sweeping the steps with a broom who quite glared at me. And so I rushed on then, into Foulsham!

It was so cold out there. Hadn't felt it at first, so cold out from the factory, cold like I'd never be warm again. Steam out of my mouth, like I was an engine. How I missed my physic then, what I should have done for a spoonful. But I was free, I was out. There were tumbled down houses and not many people about, not that early. The sun up now, but only just, doing its best to break through. I could hear the waste heaps in the distance, waves of it smashing against the wall. There was ash in the air, and soot.

I hid behind a gloomy hut. I tugged off the clothes, ripped off all Cruickshanks' things and stood in my own togs, myself again. I had no shoes, I'd forgotten to bring them. It did not matter much. Most of the children of Foulsham I had seen from my window had no shoes or wore rags on their feet. I ripped some of Cruickshanks' dress and tied myself some shoes from them. There I was then, out of it, away from Bayleaf House! All I wanted at first was to get me as far from that great factory as I may, so I just stumbled along, not looking in anyone's face, not daring to, just making progress. I would have to ask questions, get directions. I knew that I must. I had my half sovereign in my pocket. I held onto it. I warmed it. It felt a little like company. Perhaps this sov was a person once after all. Only how could that ever be so, that was some fancy surely? Oh my own sov, whatever and whoever, I'm that glad to have you.

Here I was then, back again in what was Filching and is now Foulsham.

There I was at last.

I plunged in. I told myself, go on, make a meal of it. I turned a corner and entered more populated streets, rough people in dirty clothes sitting in gutters, rag children running around, so different to how I was, so dirty. I walked on, less and less happy. I hadn't thought I'd stick out so. Despite my rag feet, I was too well dressed for them. People everywhere looked up at me. I didn't fit in, I didn't belong there. And yet I could hardly go back.

'Can I help you?' someone said.

And rather than answering I turned and ran.

'What's up with him?'

'Up to no good.'

'What's he done then, to make him run like that?'

People came after me, more of them, calling out, 'Who are you? What's your name? Stop a moment. Stop and have a word with us. Not the Tailor himself, are you? Hey, Nice Togs!

Come and talk to us.'

Children got up and followed me, finding the whole business delightful, running and skipping after me, singing,

Spit spat sputum,
Whither are you walkin',
Forlichingham Mound
You are bound.
Crick crack sternum
You shall fall in.
Slip and trip and smack your head
Foulsham Mound, that's your bed.

I knew that song. I felt in my head that I knew it, that I had sung it myself as a child, no doubt skipping along these same dirt streets. Help me, oh help me. There must have been twenty of them and more coming along after me.

'Leave me alone!' I called, but still they followed. My way was blocked suddenly by a tall gruff man in a battered hat.

'Have you got something?' he said. 'Something I'd want? Do you? Have you? What have you got? We share here in Foulsham, give it me. Hand it over. I mean to have it. Who says it's yorn when it's mine all along.'

A huge ugly hand was put out, and I pretended to search my pockets, but then I bent down and I sprinted for all I could into a different street.

'It's mine!' I heard the man call. 'Whatever he has it's mine! Grab 'im! Take that fat child down!'

There was a house in front of me now with a crooked

chimney pouring smoke from it. There was writing on the window, FOULSHAM PIESHOP. And in there I rushed. People at rickety tables in the half-light of the smoky room. Everyone looked around when I came in. I shut the door behind me. There were the grubby children peering in at the window. I couldn't go out there, I shouldn't go out there. I'd stop here a while. I'd stop here and catch my breath and after a time those children were certain to get bored, then I'd step out, but not a moment before.

A very skinny girl with a filthy apron came up to me.

'Do you know the House of Rats?' I asked.

'What are you havin'?' she asked.

'I'm sorry,' I said, 'truly I am. I don't mean to disturb, but do you –'

'Don't care about your sorriness. No interest in it. What are you havin'?'

'I *am* hungry,' I said, 'and that's the truth. I haven't had breakfast, I've usually had breakfast by now.'

'Quite a regular one, are you then?'

'Yes, I suppose, yes I am.'

'What are you havin'? Can't stay here if you're havin' nought, don't cater for that lot. Got any money have you?'

'Yes, yes I have.'

'So then, sit you down and for the fiftieth time, what are you havin'?'

'What have you got?'

'Pies!' she bellowed as if there were no other way to utter the word, and she followed it with one even louder, 'Buns!'

'Yes,' I said, 'a bun, please, thank you, and a pie.'

'Well then, hand it over, nothink for nothink.'

'What?' I asked.

'Your lolly, you clown. Pay first, pie follows after. That's how it is, if not you'll be back out with your chums there. They look most eager for it.'

'I need to find the House of Rats,' I said, 'I'm looking for my family, for the Haywards, do you know them? Could you give directions? Could you tell me? Hayward. House of Rats. Most urgent.'

'What's the rush? Done something have you?'

'No, no, I haven't. No rush, no rush. It's just . . . do you know the House of Rats?'

'Certainly I do, but sit you down have something to eat first, then I'll tell you anything. That's if you have any money.'

'I do have money.'

'So you says.'

'Though I'd rather not spend it.'

'And that's a common enough sentiment. E'en so, cough up!'

I put my hand in my pocket. I felt my half sovereign there. Held on to it.

'I've no time for this,' she said. 'I'll set Charley on you and he's a brute. Charley! We've one that won't pay here, he needs tossing out. Charley!'

In the background, from a room quite full of steam, a very large shape began to stir.

'No,' I said, 'please, miss, not to be so hasty. I said I have money and here it is indeed. Here.' I took it out, out in the open. The wretched girl looked down at it, she lay her hand out flat.

'This is my money,' I said.

'That'll cover it,' she said. 'More than cover it several times over.'

'It's a half sovereign,' I said.

'So I see,' she said.

'It's my half sovereign,' I said. 'My particular half sovereign.'

'Is it though?'

'I'm to look after it.'

'Loyalty's first to your stomach, I always say.'

'I'm never to spend it.'

'Shan't do nothing for you if you don't.'

'It's mine you see.'

'No,' she said, 'you're wrong there. Mine now.'

She had it in her own filthy hand then.

She was walking away with it.

My sovereign!

Why did I feel so sad of a sudden? Why was I crying, the tears coming so fast?

My own sov!

My bloody sov!

Binadit

2

DEEPDOWNSIDE

The narrative of the Former Ward of the
Borough of Forlichingham, no longer resident
at that address, disposed, thrown out into
the heapland

I found it and so it is mine. Takes one such as me to find such
a thing as that. I scrambled upwards. Hadn't been on top for
many a day. The weather had been so miserable that it wasn't
safe to go up, so I lived under, in the dark. I sees in the dark
and am comfortable enough there. I live under, in the deeps.
I knows it, knows it well. Sometimes, when I get the fancy, I
surface. I find me a spot, a place to perch, and I sing out. I cry
out. I groan and whoop and make my big noise.

'Binadit!' I screams. 'Binadit! Binadit!'

That's what I sound most. That's much of my vocabulary.
They threw me out here in the Heaps, sent me out over a mile
in distance and left me here to drown. But you can't sink me.

I'm made of such stuff I am. I survive. I live out in the Heaps and have grown big on it. I'm twice the size I was before who was already much. They're frightened of me, those indoor dwellers, terrified of me. Whenever they catch sight of me they run inside for cover. I'm the outdoors, I am.

I made a deal with the objects. We're one. We're of a piece, me and the wastelands. We're familiar. Intimate. The people from over the wall don't spot me mostly, lumbering in their distance. I'm invisible to them. I'm every piece of rubbish. I can be big. I can be monstrous as a mountain when I call all the rubbish to me, and it plays and throws around me and we are BIG BIG!

I'm everywhere all about.

You can't see me.

Here I am.

But where was I? I move in my mind about from bit to bit. I'm no constant thinker, I tell a bit of this a bit a that. I'm as varied as the Heaps, which to the unfamiliar observer is only brown and greyish, but to me is a kaleidoscope of experience. I move from object to object and with it shifts my mind, roll me over, lift a cover, drag out a bone: I'll tell you another story. Binadit am I. 'Tis home. 'Tis mine. I found it! There we are again! That was it. I found it! And so it's mine. Wot is it? Nothing much you might say, but I knows it. I feel it's good. I take it, I grab at it and hold it to me safe, and quick down I take it, deep deep under where I sleep in the deeps. Drowned dead. I am rubbish. Yes, yes, but wot is it? The new thing?

Wot?

I didn't say again?

No, I never.

Dumb old Binadit, foolish old Binadit, wobbly old Binadit, forever moving on, living heap, man of filth, heaphead, idiot, idiot. Meant to say. Well, I'll tell you then, I mean to.

Didn't say again.

Wot again?

No, you never.

Well then, here it is:

A clay botton.

My clay botton.

I found it.

I've a nose for it, always have had. I know your fresh filth from your old filth, I knows new stinks from ancient stunk. I can smell a mile off. I knows it, I feels it. I hop about upon the surface rummaging here and there finding my grubbing. I love it, I love it, it's all my living. Picking it up, putting it in, swallowing, sometimes sicking it back up, not often. I do digest most things. Rubber, cloth, rich pickings for me they are, metal sometimes. I like the slice of it, like blood it is.

But so, there I was up above after the big winter storm and out in the sunlight, and moving me here and there seeing wot's come up, wot's new, a bit of this a bit a that. Have a bite of seagull. That I will, thank you very much. Maybe I'll catch me a rat, alive or dead doesn't much signify. Iron gut, that's wot I am. Mister Eat All, ever have been. And there it was, very near the top. I picked it up, a botton, a clay botton, so wot? So very much. I like bottons. I keep bottons, shiny or dull. I'll have the lot. I've got me a tin Deepdownside and in that tin

I keep my bottons. I smelt the clay botton, put it to my old nozzle, those sniffing tunnels of mine. Where'd you come from? And I looks up and I sees the House way over yonder and I says, you're from there, from that ugly heap, the foul heap, the big blood heap, the spit heap, the dung heap, that heap of heaps where the real filth is, that's where you've been, ain't you? You've been tossed out. Why did they? Wot did you do? You're a botton, you are. Why do they hate you so? Well, I'll have you, little thing. Come under. Come down. Come deep down into the darks. My botton. Come along.

Past. Future. Present. Wot's that to me? Every day for me is like the one before it, just as much the one after it. They tumble in on each other. I can't tell any from the other. It may as well be a Tuesday as a Friday. I see times of the year only when I come up. Sometimes I'm down so long the season's shifted while I've been in the dark places eating my fill of the ooze at the bottom, where the black rivers run, and I hadn't noticed the spring come till I saw the flowering weeds growing out of the dirts. We do got flowers here, even here they shall grow. There's beauty for you. Tenacious, beauty is, you can't blot it out.

Deep down where I live with me, there's no summer and no winter. There's no Mondays or Sundays. We don't do Christmas or Michaelmas or Candlemas or Martinmas, never no Lent, never was an Easter to speak of. All's the same down deep in the dark, all year, day and night, all the same, and down here, down below in the thick black of it, it's always the same temperature, never varies. Down here, at this depth, down here in Deepdownside (my address, that is, my castle, my shed, my lean-to, my kingdom, my box, my place), in the thick black, deep black, pitch black, black black.

Down here the creatures alongside me, the deep ones, are all blind. Little white eyes. There are rats deep down here and white things which once upon a time were perhaps seagulls but now are closer to fish than birds, all blind. There's no use in seeing this deep under, no future in it. Sometimes I think I might go blind, and that didn't use to worry me much, but every now and then I have a fancy to see a thing and then I clamber up, gets harder to go all the way up there. I heaves and pushes and eats my way up and then how the light stings. After a while all that terrible light spooks me, the great height of sky, the cold bigness of it, and back down I go into the darkness. It's constant, it's peace, it's forgetting: it's home.

Home is a big metal room, was a huge safe room from a banking house that went bust and was thrown out, the whole jimmy of it. That's where I keep me deep under, with drawers and treasures, sharp and soft and crackling and spiking and dead and forgot and rescued and remembered and this and that I have for my liking, to stroke or to eat or to have for company. My home.

Was home.

Not no more.

Not the same after, was it? It was home but home was taken from me, different afterwards, suddenly very different. After I found the clay botton time came back to my life. I began to remember. I thought of things I hadn't thought of for years in the dark. I joined candlestubs collected and made me light below, hadn't had light down there for so long.

They called me 'It'.

I am It.

It of the Heaps.

Wot thoughts! All because of that newest botton. And then I seem to know streets and leaning buildings. I remember people just over the wall, people on the edge of Lundin, and another wall keeping them in in their turn. For they are not loved either. The Lundin ones think them horrible and build a wall 'tween them, and they think the Heaps horrible and build a wall to keep Heaps away. So much walling there is. Filchin', the place is called. Filchin', the town between the walls. One wall keeps Lundin away, the other keeps the Heaps out. Heaps! Heaps! How they fear them! And something else I know: I was born out here in the Heaps. It was my own mother, the Heapland was, a loving mother to me. That other mother, she that bore me, flesh mother, she that tried to poison me inside her, she left me out here in the Heaps, hoping I'd never be seen by anyone. Didn't happen, did it? She left a little token, a scratch on scrap tin. BINADIT read the wobbly hand. She must a done it after I was born, made the name with some hair claps or shard of glass or rusting nail. Put it there, my own name in faint hand, BINADIT. And beneath that, RIP. Only I didn't rip, no, no I didn't. Why did you not want me, Mother? Why did you leave me there? I wasn't alone though. Heaps, heaps all about me, the Heaps they protected me, they fed me. I don't like to remember.

Didn't think of it till the botton.

Why does that botton make me remember so?

I curse that botton then. I hate it and want it gone. I want to forget! It hurts me so to remember. I'll smash it, I tell myself. I'll stamp upon it, I'll crush it. I'll eat it, I'll crunch it and then it shan't come again ever more.

Oh a botton, a botton! A botton's a thing!

I have such other lovely bottons. Bottons that never did me no harm. Brass bottons with anchors, brass bottons with crowns, mother-a-pearl bottons, tin bottons, embordered bottons. Bottons, pretty bottons. Not that clay botton, not pretty one bit.

'Orrid botton.

Wot it has done to me? I was happy enough before now.

'Binadit!' I shout at it in my darkness. 'Binadit!'

I put my fist out. I mean to thump it. I want to see it broken and rubbed into dust. I want to see it hurting. I strike a flint against a wall. I fire up my candlemess. Not enough. Spluttering sun. There too I have a little paraffin salvaged, but once in a rare while I flint it alight. There, how the flame makes the botton looks like it's dancing, makes it looks like it's shifting from side to side. I'll crush it!

'Binadit!' I howl. I screams at it. I shake the light at it.

That thing dances, that 'orrible botton thing. It shifts and flips, and makes a dance all of its own. It's just the light upon it, it's only the flames that are wobbling so. I hold the light still. The light steadies but the botton doesn't. It flips and turns and makes a general nuisance of itself.

A botton dancing in the dark.

Hold you now! Stop that!

But it don't, not a bit. It flips and spins on, spins faster and faster and seems in fact to grow. A great botton. Wot will you do, shall you do damage unto me? I am the one to doubt it. I hate the botton then, I'm frightened of it. It stretches and twists and moves until it is no longer botton shape at all, and there in my dim light is something else.

Not botton no more.

It's a great rat.

No, it isn't.

'Tis.

Is not.

It's a person-thing. It's a person, an unleathered person. When did I last see a person out of leathers? This one in a thin black dress. So much pink! Then I think, then I have it: I'll eat it. Yes, I'll eat it. It's very fresh. But then that thing, that person-thing, it shifts in its place and looks out and then it makes a noise. It says some sounds that I cannot make any sense of. It says the same sound over and over and then at last I think I have it. I seem to have it in my head, a new sound sitting beside my Binadit. This is the call it makes, here it is, very fast,

'Loosypinnnnott.'

Eh wot?

'Loooseee Pennnint.'

Eh?

'Lucy Pennant.'

A Serving Girl, a Thief, a Chemist

3

ODYSSEY OF
A HALF SOVEREIGN

Beginning the narrative of Clod Iremonger,
formerly of Forlichingham Park, London, moved
to Bayleaf House, Forlichingham, stolen from
that place

Bound and Round

Am I dead now? I think I may be dead. I am not a person, that much is certain, though I do so remember being one. I think I am a thing. I think I have been stuck in this thing-prison for some time, I cannot tell how long. Yet suddenly I can think more. I can feel more. I can hear, such new hearing, not the small and vague whispering of before, now I catch real sounds, all about me. I have been dropped in a dark place, there are many other things beside me, some of them make little noises.

'Elsie Protherow.'

'Teddy Newbolt.'

'Joseph Turner.'

'Ida Goldenbaum.'

'How do?'

'Welcome.'

'Morning to you.'

Little lost voices trembling in the dark. I was huddled next to other things, heaped among them. I heard their mutterings.

'Who's there?'

'Someone new?'

'Is newness? Some new story?'

'Tell us, tell us!'

'We'll tell you ours.'

'It's only friendliness.'

'If you tell us yorn.'

'Just being social.'

'Who first?'

'I'll go. I was a boy once. Was a good boy I was, was useful,' came a small voice. 'I was needed. I slunk about with the sifting lads in the heaps, top wave, that was me, but then I slipped and got a cut and then the Iremonger foreman he came for me. He pulled me from the line. Took me down a back way. He says, show me your cut and I shows it. And he says, "Well then, what are you worth? Eat this, it will make you useful." And then, suddenly I am on the floor, not Jos Turner that I was before but now only this ha'penny bit.'

'Tha's as nothing,' came another. 'My own brother Porky – so named cos he was but skin and bone – he wot used to work one of the sump pumps. A cold came into his lungs and took up

42

permanent lodging there. No matter how he tries to persuade it out, it stays on. So my bro Porky, getting thinner all the while, though you shouldn't think it possible, he coughed and hacked and spat red poor boy he does, and then an Iremonger he comes along and says, "Well, Pork, I reckons you needs a rest, don't ye?" And I never saw Porky again but that Iremonger when he came by he had some lead piping with him that was never there before. For myself, they just asked me my age and looked at my teeth. Eat this they say, and then all of a suddenly here I am, coin of the realm. Penny am I, though once I was Phil Bishop, please to remember.'

'Tuppence, am I called,' a different voice began. 'Though once was counted little Jenny Northam. My mam and dad they turned over one morning into glazed tiles. Cannot say how it had happened, yet I knows it was them. I called out, screaming through the district. "Look what's come of them, my own mam and dad!" and an Iremonger he sidles up and says, "Poor girl, let me help you now, give over the tiles. Have this to suck on, it shall make you good and useful." And I don't know if I'd given the tiles before I turned tuppence. I don't know, and if I didn't, did I then drop Mam and Dad? Did I shatter them?'

Such stories, stories in the darkness.

'And you, you new round, what have you to say?'

There was a silence.

'Come now, Shiner, cough it up. Let's hear from you.'

Only silence.

'I thought as much. Stuck up, that one, all shut up.'

Then something occurred to me.

'Excuse me,' I said.

'Oh, but now he speaks!'

'I can speak!' I cried.

''Course you can. Whatever did you think?'

'And you can hear me!'

'Not fast, not a very quick one, are you?'

'Hello, hello!' I said. 'Hello one and all!'

'Morning.'

'Morning. How do you do?' I cried.

'Polite for a half sov, ain't you?'

'All the half sovs and sovs I ever knewed before, they'd never talk.'

'Not to such as us.'

'We haven't had such as you in here afore. I've seen sovs, but when I was in the counting house. Not 'ere, though, not in such a place as this.'

'Excuse me,' I added, 'and forgive me if I am but slow as you say – am I to understand, am I to believe, that I am here among you all, in a drawer perhaps, and that we are all, to think of it, we are all coins?'

Laughter from the coins then, grim laughter.

'Excuse me,' I continued, 'could you tell me then, if you shouldn't mind overly much, if you might inform me how one, well . . . stops being a coin.'

No laughter then.

'You are green, aren't you,' came a voice at last. 'You're a coin now, and you stay a coin, for always till you run down, that's how it is. I'm Willy Mead that was, a penny now. One minute here one minute there, in a pocket out a pocket, through and through, I've been all over Foulsham I have. I was once out

Kentish way, nearly had me up to Scotland, but I was back here again. Foulsham once more, got dented, so I'll likely keep here now. I'm good for a half pie in this shop, equal to a bun, am I. I'm the poor person's friend. I hungered once, when I was a boy, thought I'd run for it, out of Foulsham, took my chances. I got over the London wall, with rope, that was all. Heaved me up in the night, and then dropped me down the other side, and run in. Out of Foulsham and into London itself.'

'What a thing!'

'What a story!'

'I come down hard enough the other side,' the coin continued, 'but they didn't catch me, not at first. They heard me though, came running after. They caught up with me down the Old Kent Road. They found me soon enough, they knew I was from Foulsham, could tell in an instant. Didn't want our type there. Gave me a beating so's I knew it. Thought I shouldn't survive it but I did. Sent me back.'

'They'd shoot you for that now.'

'And that's the truth. There are soldiers the other side of the London wall, and if you so much as put your head over, then they pop you off. Only last week someone was shot trying. Only the carts of rubbish can come in and out, and how they're searched when they leave empty. No, there's no use in trying, can't get over.

'I was but ten years old when the London constabulary returned me to Foulsham,' concluded the coin. 'Some Iremonger, he took charge and pennied me. Not so much to worry over is there now. I'd rather be a penny. I been about now well enough! I've been beyond!'

'Oh! Oh!' I cried. 'What you have known and felt!'

'Don't pity us, do you?'

'Do you?'

'He pities us!'

'Who's he to pity?'

'No, no,' I said, 'I'm just . . . I'm just so new to this. You know so much and, in truth, I so very little. I should very much like to learn. Are we lost then, quite lost?'

'What a baby you are! Fresh minted I'd say. You don't know nothing of anything, do you?'

'Not much I suppose,' I said.

'I've seen the Tailor, the Tailor himself! I was in his pocket awhile.'

'No!'

'You don't say!'

'Oh, but I do say!'

'The Tailor?' I asked. 'Who is the Tailor, if you please?'

All gasped at me as if I'd said something quite unfathomable. Something of quite considerable ignorance.

'You are dumb, ain't you? Been sitting in silk pockets I shouldn't wonder. You spent so long amongst worsted and tweed that you don't know nothing of the real world, you're that cushioned. Well, buck up, lad! You're in Foulsham now, prepare to get dirty. I don't know how you made it here, but now you're here amongst us you'll get good and scratched.'

'I'm sure I shall,' I said, 'and I'm glad of your teaching. Who, please to tell, is the Tailor?'

'WANTED FOR MURDER. That's who. Him who the posters are all about, all of them with his name on it. He's the spanner in the machine. He goes to a person with sharp scissors and he cuts at them and they all spill out. He's here in Filching. Around us e'en now. Thick among us. He's in every corner, and yet no one ever catches him.'

'Is he really true, this Tailor?' I asked.

'Certainly! Who asked you anyway, you great shiny bit? Who's talking to you? Who are you to interrupt our meeting?'

'How you do talk on so,' I said. 'I've never heard such talking from objects before.'

'Money's always talking, you yella lump. We're always moving here and there, ever being spent, going from hand to hand, from place to place. We know more than anyone, we do. We see far more. We get about, we rootless ones. Everyone needs us, everyone wants us. But how comes you don't know that? What were you anyway before you spruced up a sovereign?'

'Yes, come on. We'll have your story. What were you?'

'Just a moment ago,' I said, 'I began to understand that I was in James Henry Hayward's pocket. He was supposed to look after me. I've always been with James Henry, all my life, but now, it seems, we have become separated.'

'You've been spent,' some coin said.

'I've been spent?' I asked.

'Yes, yes, you've been spent, you have.'

'But why? Whatever for?'

'For buns, I shouldn't wonder, and for pies.'

'He's spent me for a bun, for a pie?' I asked. 'Why would he do such a thing?'

'You're worth many pies and buns you are. You're all of a feast you are, with trimmings on the side. Because of you we lost half the drawer in change. There was a shilling giving us an excellent story before he was pulled out on a cause a you. So then, make up for it why don't you. What's your name? We like a story we do; we'll spread it yonder all about here and there, sow it we shall. Come on then, give over. Your tale, your bit of property.'

'Before I was a sovereign?' I asked.

'A half sovereign!' called a penny. 'Don't get above yourself.'

'Yes, quite right thank you. Before I was a half sovereign I was called Clod.'

'Clod? What sort of a name is that. Clod? That don't have the making of a half sovereign if you ask me.'

'I lived in a big house with my family. I could see Filching.'

'Foulsham we call it now, Foulsham since all the stinking black smoke came to us. Falling over the town.'

'I could see Foulsham as you call it,' I resumed, 'in the distance, though I'd never been there, not actually. I wanted to . . .'

'Well you're here now, ain't you, chicken.'

'In the thick of it, ain't you.'

'Clod? That's not a name. What was your real name?'

'Clodius,' I said. 'Clodius Iremonger.'

That stopped them. They all suddenly clammed up. Not another murmur from any of them. Silent coins, as if that's all they were, just coins, nothing more than coins, not coins made of turned people.

'Hallo,' I said. 'Hallo, talk with me won't you? I knew someone from Filching. She was called Lucy Pennant. Have any of you heard of her? Come along, please. I do implore you.

Lucy Pennant. She has red hair and is freckled all over. Do you know her? Might you help me? Please talk to me, please don't shut up so.'

But they never made another sound.

The drawer was opened now and then and light was amongst us a moment, but I was not taken out. Other coins were and different ones plopped down in their place, and whenever a new one arrived, there was a quick warning call from the coins,

'Iremonger! Among us!'

And then afterwards only silence.

I don't know how long I was in the drawer but at last dark fingers plucked me out. I was rubbed on an apron and taken away.

The Thief

I was shoved in a pocket and taken from what I understood was a pieshop, out I supposed into Forlichingham, or Foulsham as they seemed to call it now.

I was happy to be away from all those grim coins, though I supposed it must mean I was further away from James Henry. How far away from each other must we be before we both begin to suffer? I remembered then – everything rushing back to me – the poor wretch Alice Higgs, and Aunt Rosamud's agony at losing her. There must be so many people lost from each other all over London, all those broken people, half people, missing their object, or lonely people not knowing why they feel so incomplete. And then, on top, all those people not people any more, all those people tumbling into things, and then no one to love them any more, no one to know who they are.

There were such noises, such noises on the way! I heard them all, louder, ever louder: the cries of all the objects. Such calling from the things of Foulsham.

'I was Georgie Brown afore now, here I am a boot scraper.'

'Can you hear me? I'm a wicker basket!'

'Me, me, I'm a flat cap.'

'On the ground, over yonder, you hear me, I am a milk churn. Was Eve Bullen before time.'

'Wheelbarrow, wheelbarrow, I was Edvard Pedersen.'

'Am a sandwich board. I boast ALLBRIGHT'S ARTIFICIAL TEETH but before I was known Archie Stannard.'

'I am a tooth! Am a false tooth what once was Annie Pugh.'

'Oh, I'm a shoe now!'

'A belt! A belt!'

'Here I am Hamilton Foote but you shall not recognise me, I'm string only.'

'I hear you!' I cried. 'I hear you all, poor devils that you are!'

'He hears us!'

'He hears us!'

In a moment there were less voices, we'd moved somewhere more remote. I was suddenly out in the open again – the bakery girl, she can't have been more than fifteen, her black fingers were holding me up to someone else. Such light, I could see, I could see out and see clear. But now I was out and seeing and remembering more it seemed to me I heard in some new and strange way that I hadn't before. Was it, perhaps, being an object that made me hear all the greater? There was a noise of something wailing somewhere, not words, just sounds, sounds like a new language, like something I'd never heard before. A naked strange sound, coming, I thought, from the girl, from deep within. How to explain it? There was a sound inside her wailing, so I understood it, that made the noise, 'Thimble.'

This girl was showing me to some shaven headed man in thick dirty leathers, he had that other sound about him too, but deeper and quieter. I heard it though, it said, 'Steaming iron.'

'I brought it,' she said.

'Give it up then,' said the brute.

'First you must give me back the candlestick you stole, the one that I think my mother became. You said you should, for a half sovereign, well I have it now. But I want the candlestick. You must return it, it's my ma I think.'

'I see the coin, but I don't feel it. Hand over.'

'The candlestick, I'll have the candlestick first.'

'The half sov.'

I was passed over to thick crude hands, fingers sausage thick, and scarred and scuffed.

'Now the candlestick,' she said. 'I must have it.'

'Where'd you come by this anyhow, so great a sum? Did you steal it?'

'It's from a customer.'

'Likely story. Who've you been entertaining in your slophouse?'

'Please, please, the candlestick.'

'Thimble,' came the noise from within her again, though

51

louder this time.

'Who did you steal this from? You've lifted it from the till, I reckon. But hold on a minute now, hold back. Something is coming to me, yes it is. It looks familiar it does, now it seems I recollect it, I reckon it was mine all along and you filched it from me.'

'Please, no, please, give me that candlestick, it's all I want.'

'You little thief.'

'I did not steal it! Please, I'm begging you.'

'Don't you touch me, you cutpurse. I'll call an Iremonger on you, just you see if I don't.'

'Where's the candlestick? WHERE?'

'Oh, let off! It's gone, hasn't it! Such a fuss over a candlestick. I sold it on a week ago. Now get off me or I swear I'll hit you so hard you won't wake till next week.'

'Who did you sell it to? Where?'

'I'm bored on this now, get lost.'

'Thimble,' came the under voice.

'Ma! Ma! My own ma!'

'Shut it, or I'll strike.'

'Give me my money back.'

'Money, what money are you talking about? Never was none that I recall.'

'My half sov!'

'Don't know what you mean.'

'Please! Don't do this! Please!'

'Thimble.'

'Help! Help me!'

'Thimble!'

'I'm not touching you.'

'Help, oh help me!'

'I tell you I'm not touching you!'

It took but a moment and on the ground just where the girl had been standing before was a mere thimble. The poor little object let off a little steam on the ground, as if it were quite hot. Then I heard it whisper,

'Annie, I'm Annie Nelson. Help me. Please help me.'

'God 'ave mercy,' the thief said, shaking himself as if he had a sudden ague, he ground the thimble in the mud with his boot, pushed me deep down into his leather pocket and rushed off.

The Chemist

The next I knew, I was being taken out again, out into the light and passed on to another hand. I was in a different shop. There were jars of strange things all around and, hanging from hooks in the ceiling, many dried herbs. There were new voices from objects calling out, they seemed to start shouting from every corner.

'Chas Butler.'

'Josef Singer.'

'Anushka Dugal.'

'Olive English.'

'Francis Sullivan.'

'Help me, I'm a bell jar!'

'Over here! I'm Patrick Leary the tongue compressor. Help us, you can help us!'

'Please! Please help! I'm a bleeding pan!'

Those unhappy sounds were drowned by the thief addressing the chemist, 'I need me some grinding for my pipe. I've ever such a headache.'

The thief seemed very distracted and the noise inside him, 'Steaming iron', that much more confident.

'Yes, sir,' said the man behind the dusty counter. 'Seven and six, or ha'p'orth.'

'Ha'p'orth.'

'I'll make the measure.'

'Don't you fix it mind. I know your scales. Be generous, will you?'

'Steaming iron.'

'I shall be exact, sir. Your money first.'

'Here.'

I was upon the counter.

'So much?'

'Come on. I've paid you ain't I?'

'Where did you get that?'

'What's that to you?'

'Steaming iron, steaming iron.'

'A little moment, sir.'

The chemist picked me up then, looked at me hard, and next I know I am between his yellow teeth and he is biting me for proof that I'm real.

'It's proper,' the thief said.

'Yes, it does seem so. Only thing is it isn't legal.'

'Not legal, what are you saying? You're trying to thieve me.'

'No, indeed sir, you may see the posters all about the streets,

54

fresh glued it's true, but all stating that half sovereigns are no longer legal tender in Filching.'

'I need some grinding; I've such an ache for it!'

'I'm sure we can come to some accommodation.'

'I've such a pain of a sudden. A gnawing pain.'

'Steaming iron, steaming iron.'

'Yes, yes, of course sir. I don't mean to cast aspersions, but you never can be too sure, can you?' said the chemist.

'Come now, oh my head, my head!'

'Are you quite well, sir?' the chemist asked, standing back from the thief.

'Quick with the medicine! I've never known such pain.'

'Steaming iron, steaming iron.'

'I must be careful, the right amount,' said the chemist, looking at the thief most particularly and standing further back.

'Help me now, help me can't you?'

'Can I?'

'STEAMING IRON, STEAMING IRON.'

'Any moment now, I think, sir,' said the chemist to the thief, 'and you'll be off.'

'Any minute what? What are you saying? Off I go where? My head!'

'STEAMINGIRONSTEAMINGIRON!'

'Goodbye, sir, I thank you for your custom,' said the chemist.

'My h—' but the thief could not finish his sentence, his face suddenly stiffened and in a terrible instant grew grey and shrivelled up solid and landed with a loud and unsettling clang upon the floor. Thief no more.

'Well, well,' said the chemist, leaning over his counter. 'What have we here? Is it of any use?'

With the aid of a pair of fire tongs from his hearth he lifted this new hot object – formerly a thief – beside me on the counter. It gave off heat and whispered very faintly, 'Billy Stimpson.'

'Sir,' said the chemist, 'you are now a steaming iron. I daresay I may sell you to the Iremonger washers themselves. You'll be losing the creases off their starched shirts no doubt. A quality item you are, most useful. Most grateful. I may get a bargain for you, and besides, here is this to boot: a half sovereign. Most kind, most generous. Thank you, Mr Iron, you are most excellent for business.'

I was pushed into the chemist's pocket. I heard a door open and shut. I was outside again. Objects calling out up and down the street.

'A tin spoon now, was William Wilson.'

'I was Janet Bolton once.'

'Joanna Thompson, I was, I was.'

A Family by the Fire

When I was taken out once more, I was in a very different place. There were cages all about, busy people making things. Cages hung from the ceiling, cages all about the floor. And basins and sinks, and troughs. Objects called out again,

'I'm here a cage, I used to be Mabel Taylor.'

'I was Cyril Cronin. I don't want to be a gluepot. Can anyone help me?'

I was handed over.

'I can't take the half sovereign,' someone was saying. 'It isn't safe.'

'You may have it in exchange for a tanner's worth of rat. Now there's a deal you don't see every day.'

'Not such a deal if I'm found with such a coin upon me.'

'Then hide it, keep it safe until the search is over.'

'I've a family to think of.'

'You have indeed. When did you last see such money?'

'I cannot deny it has been a while.'

'Hasn't it! Hasn't it! Do look at the coin, Herbert Arthur! Look at it shining. Think what you may buy for that.'

'Nothing now, half sovereigns are not allowed in Foulsham. They are to be turned over.'

'Nothing now perhaps, but so much later.'

'Come, come, two pound of rat is all I'm asking.'

'For an illegal coin, it's not much of a bargain.'

'Oh look, Father,' said a young woman. 'A whole half sovereign! May I hold it?'

'No, Sarah Jane, you're not to touch it. It isn't safe.'

'Oh look,' said an older woman. 'Will you look at that, a half sovereign!'

'Please to look,' said the chemist. 'Please to. Have a feel, do.'

I was then handed around all the people in that small factory. A young man had me, he passed me to the youngest, Sarah Jane, and she in her turn handed me to the wife and thence I was held by a very old woman lacking several of her fingers. And what fingers they all had, these people. They were so gnawn at, so bullied and scarred.

'Come, come,' said the chemist, 'have you ever seen such

a coin? You may consider yourself rich. You could buy things, purchase new tools, put something by. We have such little to hold onto, we people of Foulsham. We must make do with what we have; we must grab at chances when they come our way. We are under Iremonger tenancy, all of us. What are we to do, Umbitt owns us. We are his property after all. We must only be cunning and fight for our crust of bread, and when help is offered, then we must take it, and be grateful of it. Now, tell me, how is business? Does it thrive?'

'Indeed, I must say it does not.'

'The truth, justly spoken. So then, my offer is a blessing on this house. Come now, what do you say?'

'I say we should, Father,' said Sarah Jane.

'We must all be agreed on this,' said the father. 'Everyone must agree. We'd be hiding it. If it were found there'd be no mercy.'

'Oh, Herbert Arthur, it might save us,' said the wife. 'We'll keep it.'

'It may also, my dear Agnes Nancy, be our death.'

'Well, Pa,' said the young man, 'I think we should chance it. We've known Mr Griggs these many years. He shan't rat on us, so to speak.'

'No, indeed,' said the chemist, Griggs by name as I now understood, 'not I. You know me. Young William Henry speaks true.'

It was then that I heard the undervoice of the chemist calling. It came up like a wind from deep within him, 'Hairnet.'

'There's a reward for anyone who correctly informs on those who are shielding half sovereigns,' said the father.

'What's that to me? Why should I do such a thing? The very mention of it is insulting. I need rats. Rats are necessary for my work. How often have I come to you for the buying of rats?'

'In truth, not much of late.'

'Come now, I came to do you a favour.'

'Or to collect a reward.'

'I am an honest professional. I'll take the coin back and be gone!'

'Wait!' said the mother. 'Not so fast, Mr Griggs. We'll take your coin; we'll give you the weight of varmint you require.'

'At last some sense! I've half a mind to rescind the offer.'

'Only first off,' said the mother, 'we'll have you sign a piece of writing, something that says that we come by the coin from you and the date and the time.'

'You don't trust me!'

'No,' said the father, 'that's about the size of it.'

'But I came out of kindness!'

'So then, be kind. Be kind and sign.'

'Hairnet.'

'I cannot believe you people.'

'Here we are then, Mr Griggs, please to sign.'

'I'm not certain that I shall. What's in it for me?'

'Your rats, Mr Griggs. Didn't you say you were in great need of rats?'

Mr Griggs let out an almighty belch which coincided to my hearing a loud exclamation of 'Hairnet!'

'Are you quite well, Mr Griggs?' asked Sarah Jane. 'Can we get you something?'

Again Mr Griggs exuded a mouthful of air, again with the sound 'Hairnet! Hairnet!'

'You look unwell, sir.'

'Hairnet!'

Mr Griggs was put in a chair.

'Thankee, I feel powerfully gaseous. Some trapped air I think, please to excuse. Oh, my stomach, the sharpness!'

'Hairnet!'

Mr Griggs doubled over suddenly. He tossed about on the chair like he was some small black cloud of weather. He spun and circled like black wool in a tempest, out of that mass sometime a hand appeared like it was drowning in the sea, clutching for land, and then, finally, there was no more movement and the lank black stringy thing lay docile at last upon the chair. Inevitably, a hairnet.

'I'm Jebediah Griggs. I'm not at my best, please to help.'

'The disease!' cried Sarah Jane. 'The disease has come to this house!'

'Quick, Herbert Arthur,' cried the mother, 'the tongs. In the fire with it.'

The father picked up the hairnet with a pair of rusted firetongs and pushed it into the fire. All that was left of Mr Griggs, chemist of Foulsham, sizzled mournfully, sparked a little, and was quickly consumed. The last of him a dissipating cloud of black smoke, that, judging by the reaction of the family, stank something chronic.

'What do we do now?' asked the young man. 'What do we do with the coin?'

'We hide it,' said Sarah Jane.

'We throw it away,' said the mother.

'That coin is dirt,' said the grandmother.

'Fetch the crucible,' said the father. 'We must destroy it.'

Binadit

4

MAN OF FILTH

Beginning the narrative of Lucy Pennant,
of no fixed abode

'Lucy Pennant.'

I was in a fight. I was trying to get out. I was with Clod. He couldn't hear. There was this thing, huge it was, made of many things and an old man and a teacup that the old man danced upon it until it was crushed to dust. I called out for the teacup and the old man had me launched off the ground and spinning in the air. And then nothing. Nothing at all. Then suddenly back again.

I was in the dark, very dark, huge stink. Couldn't see anything, shut in with a pig, at first I thought. I'm in a piggery. I did not know how I got there, wherever I was. I didn't know even if I was still alive at first. But I could talk. In fact I couldn't stop talking. And all I could say over and over was,

'Lucy Pennant. Lucy Pennant. Lucy Pennant.'

Couldn't stop myself, over and over.

But then in the darkness, there was that something else. Something big and dark. The pig? And it, this thing, it said,

'Binadit.'

Whatever that meant.

And I said,

'Lucy Pennant.'

And it said,

'Binadit.'

'Lucy Pennant.'

'Binadit.'

'Lucy Pennant.'

I couldn't see what was making the noise, only that it was huge and each time I said my name the thing in the dark responded 'Binadit.' It was quite close. I had no idea where I was or how I had come there.

'Binadit!'

It was getting angry, each 'Binadit' was louder than the one preceding. It was shifting in the darkness, getting closer. Well, I thought, I don't know what you are or what you want but you don't sound exactly contented, and if you shout at me then I shall shout back. No doubt you're quite a thing, no doubt you are. Well good luck to you, I thought, because I'm quite a thing and all. I shan't go without a good fight. I've seen too much already; there's not much that frightens me any more. I have not come all this way to be dinner for a great pig. In truth, this thing before me was large and unpleasant and it did frighten me, but whatever is the use of being frightened? How will that get you anywhere? So then, when next it shouted,

'Binadit!'
I bellowed back,
'Lucy Pennant!'
'BINADIT!'
'LUCY PENNANT!'

And so we shouted back and forth, and when this big thing snapped his jaws and made loud grunts well then I did the same. And when the big thing spoke his noise quieter, well then I followed likewise. And so this was our first communication and we went on sounding each other out in the darkness until at last the big thing moved and he struck at something. I pushed myself backwards on all fours waiting for it to hit, but it didn't touch me. It struck into a lamp of some kind, and the light it gave off was a great sharp pain in my eyes, I covered my face over. And when I took my hands away again, I began to see what it was in the darkness with me there. Well what can I say of it? How to picture that, that thing, that dark, looming, breathing creature before me? Never seen the like.

It was such a thing of dirt. It was all got up in rubbish. Bits of things were stuck to it and grew upon it. The hair on top of the great gross head was so matted and thick that it had become a kind of armour. Things, dark crawling insects, crawled about over it and the creature paid them no heed. Bits of different things were stuck upon it, sealed hard upon it as if a welder had smote them there. You couldn't name the things, only that they created odd, jagged shapes so that the creature seemed made head to toe of rubbish and to fit into the landscape of his home so very exactly that if it didn't move and make its sound so often, you'd think it just a mound of filth. It opened its mouth to say its word and I saw that great cavern and the rocks it kept inside it. Black and grey teeth, yellow and green. And when it opened its great head hole the outgoing stench was incredible.

'Whatever are you?' I asked.

'Binadit,' it said.

'Some sort of enormous bear, I suppose, aren't you? Some sort of beast, not one I've seen before. Something strange, grown up in filth. Whatever are you then?'

'Binadit.'

'Are you animal, vegetable or mineral? Or all three perhaps.'

'Binadit.'

'If they put you in a cage they could charge a tanner for you at Filching Fair.'

At the mention of 'cage' it seemed to grow upset, it struck the dirt floor with its paw, it brought its face closer to mine and I winced at the stench of it.

'Binadit!' it growled.

'I'm going to have to be careful with you, whatever you are. Good boy, sit you down.'

'Binadit. Binadit.'

'Is that your name then? Binadit?'

That stopped it. It looked at me most strangely then. It seemed to shake its head from side to side, some itch or pain had bothered it for certain. It must have so many pains about it.

'Binadit!'

'Binadit?' I asked. 'What are you saying? Binadit? *Benedict*! You're saying Benedict, are you? Oh my sweet lord, you're one of us, aren't you, all along? You're a person too!

'Who did this to you?' I asked. 'How long have you been here? Where are we, Benedict? Where?'

'Where?'

'Yes, where, that's it, what is all this place?'

'Under. Binadit.'

'Under, Benedict? Under what?'

'Under.' He twisted his jaw trying to make it work, to move in old, forgotten ways, it was, *he* was, trying to remember. 'Under . . . heap.'

'The heaps? Under the heaps? Buried. The heaps! How, how did we get here? How do we get out?'

'I found it. I found it and so it is mine.'

'Found what? Make sense!'

'Botton. My botton.'

'What botton? Do you mean button? What are you talking about?'

'You!' he shouted. 'You were a botton before now. I found you up top. I brought you down here, to my home, to here, my place. Deepdownside. You were a botton. But now you're not a botton. Now you're a person thing. Better a botton. Like bottons. Have bottons, box of. Want to see? My bottons? Be a botton again will you? Go on. Please. Put you in my tin I will.'

'I am not a button, Benedict. I'm Lucy Pennant. Lucy Pennant, do you hear?'

'Be a botton, please to be a botton again.'

'No, I won't. I shan't!'

'Binadit!' he snapped, a warning.

'Lucy Pennant!'

'No room for you. Not now, not like this. No tin big enough. No box that large. Don't collect what you are, no collection of . . . of girls.'

'I am not part of your collection.'

'I found you!'

'I do not belong to you!'

'But I found you!'

'I am a person!'

'Be a botton.'

'I will not!'

'You were a nice botton.'

'I need to get out of here. I need to find Clod.'

'A nice botton, but a nasty girl.'

'I'm going now. If you'll tell me how.'

'Nasty girl. Taking up all my place. Not invited! Binadit!'

'I'll go happily enough and then all will be as it was.'

'No, won't! You owe me my botton. I *found* it!'

'Please, Benedict, please, I'll find you buttons. I promise, hundreds of them. Just show me out of here, get me to Filching, then I'll –'

'Not leaving. I found you. You're mine.'

'No, no, I'm not.'

'Binadit! Binadit!'

'What do you want with me?'

'Hongry. I'm hongry.'

'You won't eat me.'

'Won't I? You're fresh. Why wouldn't I?'

'I'm a person!'

'You were a *botton*!'

'*You* are a person, Benedict. People don't eat people.'

'Rats eats rats.'

'And they are vermin. We are human, we talk.'

'Rats make noise when I eat them, I used to talking food.'

'But you don't talk rat.'

'Do talk rat. Talk rat well.'

And he made a noise then, very like a rat it was.

'Benedict, talk sense, be sensible. I'll find you wonderful food. You wouldn't want to eat me, you wouldn't. I'd taste terrible . . . I'm poisonous.'

'Then I'll sick up. I don't mind.'

'Now, I've had just about . . .'

But I stopped then, there was a sudden sharp pain in my stomach, as if all my insides were being compressed. I thought I was being turned inside out, a strange violent spasm. And then it was gone again.

'What was that?' I said. 'I felt something. It hurt!'

'Was what?'

And then there it was again.

'A pain in me, a tugging, a tearing. There it is again. Help, help me, Benedict. What's happening? Help. Help! HELP!'

Unry Iremonger

Unry Iremonger

Unry Iremonger

Unry Iremonger

Unry Iremonger

Otta Iremonger

Otta Iremonger

Otta Iremonger

Otta Iremonger

Otta Iremonger

5

PUBLIC NOTICE!!!

STOLEN:
1 HALF
SOVEREIGN

All half sovereigns are to be handed over to Iremonger
Officers without delay.
Any half sovereigns found in the personal possession of
individuals or businesses beyond 14:00 hrs this day January
12th 1876 to be considered an act of law breaking and
subject to the severest penalty.

By Order
Umbitt Iremonger, owner

In service thereof Unry Iremonger, the faceless.
In service thereof Otta Iremonger, the shifter.

Unry

I, Unry Iremonger, secreted about the people. I, Unry, the one they do not know that from young age was sent out into Filching-Foulsham to be a general spy unto them all. I, Unry, person-shifter, person of little face, born in sweat and agony with a malady most peculiar. I lost my features. I was born bald like so many but my hair never grew, not a wisp of it. When I was but five my nose came off when I was a-blowing it. It dropped clean off. Likewise my ears were gone from me by ten. First the left, then the right. I keep my eyes, which I'm uncommonly grateful for. My face is a blank. It is a canvas waiting to be drawn upon, so that faces, any faces, may be set upon mine own and that I may be, as is my choosing, any number of people.

I have noses!

I have ears for any occasion.

Wigs!

I can be anyone.

I, Unry, he in the crowd, the man sitting next to you, your old workmate, the old man coughing in the coffee house, the young boy playing with the hoop. I, Unry, am set a new task. I am on the sniff for half sovereigns and all that carry them. I'm the one to do the labour. I play all roles, and have none of mine own. I'm family; I'm Iremonger every drop. But who of my family knows me? So few, so few.

They've lost something from Bayleaf and I'm to find it. They've had Governor Idwid, blind and brilliant, move his clever ears all around. They propel him through the streets in a wheelbarrow, ordering all to be silent as they rush through, and he listens. He hangs his ears out. But he does not hear it, not yet. They move him into rooms all over the borough, shoving him in here and there at random, they say,

'Quiet! Silence! Let the Governor listen! There's something lost, something lost that must be found.'

If they have half sovereigns, these people, they've hidden them long before the hearing blindman appears. They are cunning, the people of Foulsham, cunning and numerous as rats. But I, Unry, have laid in their sweat manys the night. I know their stench; I stink of them in truth. I'll find it out; I'll have them. Unry's the one to do it.

And sure enough I, I was the one that found him.

And sure enough, and sure enough, I, Unry, I was the one that caught him up.

Plump boy in the street, crumbs down his front.

Had to be him didn't it? We don't do plump here. Maybe in Bayleaf House but not here. Here the children have ribs. So I came up to him with one of my kindest noses on, and a most pleasant set of ears and such a wig of generosity to match, some welcoming, and I says,

'Well, son, what's the trouble? I'm a friend, you look as if you need one.'

'Can you help me, please, may you?'

'Yes, yes,' I says. 'Surely I can. Tell me your troubling.'

'I've . . . I've . . . I've –' what a stammering he gives – 'I've lost my sov.'

'Poor chap,' I says. 'What a thing.'

'I spent it in the pieshop and they won't let me have it back. But I must have it; it's mine you see.'

'Of course it is,' I say. 'Come along a me.'

And he follows, the sad thing, like I was a magnet. No argument, no protest, meek I'd say, and I wander him round the corner, and there at the end of the road is the Policing Station just where it should be.

'What's that?' he says.

'It's a place,' I says. 'Keep up, lad.'

'I don't like the look of it.'

'A fine place,' I say. 'They have everything there, what are you after? Are you hungry?'

'No, no I'm not. I don't ever want to eat again.'

'Thirsty then?'

'All I want, all I need is my sov, and that is in the pieshop. Then after I have it, then I'll look for my mum and dad. Have you seen them?'

''Course I have.'

'I haven't told you their names yet.'

'I know everyone.'

'Who are you anyway?'

'And I know everywhere, keep you coming.'

'Was it you, were you the one that called me? Back then, years ago. I seem to remember it now, were you the one? I was playing truant from school. Was it you? I think it was. I think it was you. You gave me the boiled sweet, was it you who took me away?'

'Come along a me, up these stairs now, nearly there.'

'It was you, wasn't, wasn't it? Why did you do that to me?

Why did you?'
  'Just a couple more, up you go.'
  'Why did you do it, oh why did you?'
  'Through this door then, good my lad, good boy.'
  'Please, you're not to do it again, do you hear?'
  'Let me show you the way.'
  'You shan't do it again, shall you?'
  'Let me tell you your way; I know the very route.'
  What a greenhorn!

I've seen it all: Foulsham love stories in dark corners, rubbish moving when it shouldn't, a whole sweatshop catch the disease of a moment, all two hundred come tumbling down. I've even seen the Tailor's long length running through the shadows. Nearly had him. I'll have him next time. I'm getting closer. I knows my way about. I'm sitting next to you. I'm everywhere all about. You'll never know me. I'm everyone.

  Only thing that may signal me out, only way you might know me, the one part of my guise that is always the same and cannot alter. I always carry with me my umbrella. My birth object it is; can't go anywhere without it.

  I forgot to mention, the boy, the soft-edged boy, crumbs down his side. I took him in, gave him shelter. He's safe now. Very.

Otta

My bro, my big bro. He's a lovedove; he's special. Though it may take me a minute to recognise him, my own flesh, still I'm the one that will know him, only me, just me. Guaranteed. Poor Mother, poor Father, what a shock we must have been to them. The noseless, earless bald boy and his sister, the little Thing. Father, Ulung Iremonger and Mother, Moyball Iremonger, worked and met and loved one another out in Security, in the Policing Station. They were ever such clever ones for detecting things. They were ever such sharp ones for sticking their hands down throats and getting the words to come out of people. It was even there, in the hard Station, that Unry was born and then later, to their shock and worry, me, Unryotta, though I'm generally known as Otta, merely Otta. In part I think on 'cause of my having quite sharp teeth, which as a child – and if I be honest even as a grown one – I find do snap on things from time to time. They've a grip, my crushing gnashers.

I came out of Mother in the form of a shapeless hunk of flesh, but they found a mouth on me, screaming. Later I was a bottle, a cup, a pan, a chair, a pole, a box, a book, a pig, a rat, a cat, a gull, a dog, a pump, a pillow, a pot, a doorstop, a bell pull, a floorboard, a sack, a hat, a pen, a brush, a wig, and, on occasions, when I must, oh they said I must at times, a little girl. They never knew where I was; they never knew what I was. That's what comes with working with such filth, says Mama, hard to wash off after. Oh, the terror when they thought they'd thrown me out with the rubbish. How I loved to play hide and seek with them! How it made them tug their own hair out in distress. To see Mother taking hold of a kettle and saying, 'Otta! Otta, stop that this instant. You're not a baby. You're not a kettle. You're six years old now, and should know better. One day the wind will change and you'll be stuck a kettle!' Oh, the games, Unry pretending he was any number of people ('Who are you there?' says Mama. 'Ulung, there's a strange man in the Station, come quick!' Or this classic, 'Owner Umbitt, how good of you to call! Excuse me, sir, but you seem just a little shrunk.') and me being any number of things. They were better days they were, before we were of use out of doors, before we were put out in Foulsham, learning the place, noticing, shifting, finding out all sorts. But we must never declare ourselves, for if we did, they'd know us ever afterwards.

We're secret people, Unry and I. Sssh.

He's all of twenty now.

And I eighteen am.

When I'm myself, I mean really myself, which is not usual, on occasion only when I get together with Unry at the Station for a bit of a flop, or when I need to report, or when I'm called in (a certain whistle is blown) such as today. Then I'm a young woman, big of bust. I have nice legs, tall too. Maybe one day I shall find me someone to take up shop with, maybe I'll retire out in Heap House. I'd like that I think.

Today I'm told there's a half sovereign gone missing, only it's not just a half sovereign. It's an Iremonger called Clod, a very gifted Iremonger but one with a flare for disobedience, and I'm to find him, and I'm to bring him in. 'Can he shift?' I ask. 'No,' they says, 'not yet. He hasn't learnt but he has great natural knowledge of things. He must be caught.'

Well then, off I scuttle.

A door is opened, a rat runs out the door down the steps of the Station. Notice that rat, it runs faster than all the others. Notice that rat, it has round its neck or its hips, or caught up in its tail depending, a ring, a curtain ring. Know that curtain ring, that brass curtain ring, it's always upon me. I never lose it. I fix it to myself, here or there, so that it doesn't fall off. I have it somewhere about. Off I go, rat and ring. See it there! Into and under and deep within. I've been everywhere. I've been everything.

There runs a rat, over your feet maybe.

That was me.

That was I.

Otta.

Gone a-hunting.

The Hayward Family –

Rat Catchers of Foulsham

6

HAVE YOU SEEN THIS BOY?

Continuing the narrative of Clod Iremonger

Notice, Missing Boy

They sat about me, waiting and waiting. In the background the father, Herbert Arthur, was stoking up the fire. The son, William Henry, had got out the crucible and was heating it up. The room was terribly hot. The people were sweating so. All the objects all about were quieter now, whispering to each other. I did not like that, it seemed to bode no good.

'Soon,' the father said, 'soon it shall be hot enough.'

'Don't touch the coin,' said the old grandmother, 'it shouldn't do to touch. Wear thick gloves when you drop it in the pan, Bertle, don't let anyone else. It's dirty, that thing is. It's filth.'

'It doesn't look dirty,' said Sarah Jane. 'It looks golden and pretty, I like it. I cannot help it, I like it. I feel a fondness for it.'

'Don't look into it, Sarah Jane. It isn't safe,' said the mother.

'I cannot help it, Ma. It is such an object. It would be a pity to harm it, I feel that in my heart. I feel I've dreamt of this coin before, as if I somehow know it.'

'It's calling her,' the grandmother cried. 'It will get to a young 'un easy, the disease, those of weak constitution, the over-innocent, the stupid. It'll bring them down. Bertle, will you hurry now!'

The fire grew hotter and the pan on top of it shifted from black to red. The family sweated over me. I tried calling out to them, but no matter how I cried, they could not hear. Only Sarah Jane seemed to want to keep me. These were superstitious people, poor people, living on the edge. I looked about their small room where they all crammed in everything that was theirs, where they worked and where they slept in rickety bunks leant against the walls. There were no pictures on the walls such as there had been back at home in Heap House. There was a single, framed bit of needlepoint, such as probably Sarah Jane had made at school, in neat, sewed lettering with flowers surrounding it, the needlework said:

TAKE THE BABY FROM THE HEAPS
AND THE WALL SHALL FALL

The only other decoration in the whole place were bill posters pasted on here and there, I supposed, to stop up cracks. Old tattered advertisements for theatre acts:

COME FEED THE IT OF THE HEAPS!
BRING ANYTHING, HE EATS ANYTHING:

GLASS, METAL, CHINA, WOOD
MR EAT-ALL! FEED HIM YOURSELF – 2D A
SPOONFULL

But most of the bill posters were all the same, the same one
over and over:

NOTICE, LOST PROPERTY: MISSING BOY
LAST SEEN NEAR HEAPWALL MAY 14TH 1860,
5 FEET 2 INCHES, BROWN HAIR, BROWN EYES.
ANSWERS TO THE NAME

JAMES HENRY HAYWARD

JAMES HENRY, IF YOU READ THIS PLEASE COME HOME.

HAVE YOU SEEN THIS BOY? Please contact
Herbert Arthur Hayward,
HOUSE OF RATS, Old Salvage Street, Forlichingham

James Henry! James Henry! My James Henry! My plug, oh
my plug James Henry Hayward! This, this was where he came
from, this, even this, was his home! I was in James Henry's
home! Here were his beloved people! Hallo, hallo, to you! I
know James Henry, I've been with him all this time! Sixteen
years ago he was lost to these people, sixteen years since I've
been born and he's been with me. Sixteen years! Sixteen years
has James Henry been stalled, sixteen years asleep as a plug,

his sister and brother were just small children then. Now quite grown up. But James Henry's still alive, I called out to them. He's not dead, though missing these long sixteen years. Help, oh help!

Listen, Haywards, listen to me!

I've seen him, even today was I with him. He's alive and well.

I tried to tell them. I thought as loudly as I could. I screamed in my mind: just a few hours ago! You may find him yet, you may find him before anyone else does. Go, and find him, now, run to him. He's in the pieshop, at least he was there this day. Run to him quick, for I need to be with him, and he with me.

But the people couldn't hear. And those people, those sacred, dear people of James Henry's, were set upon destroying me, which would harm their missing son. They'd suffer their own boy.

Help me, oh help me.

The only person who seemed to understand anything was Sarah Jane, who sat in front of me and began to weep.

'Why ever are you crying, Sarey?' asked the mother. 'It's just a coin.'

'Is it, Ma, is it? How can you be so sure? What should have happened had James Henry been turned into a coin such as this? He may have been for all we know. And now you want to hurt him!'

'One thing I do know, my girl,' said the father sadly, 'if our James Henry should have fallen into something, it's very unlike he'd turn up a sovereign. It's not like a Hayward to be a sovereign, is it. Look on the mantelpiece at your dear grandfather, look at that beloved rubber glove and tell me that that sovereign is related in any way to that rubber glove.'

'Oh, my George Henry,' wailed the old woman of a sudden, reflecting no doubt on happier days. 'Oh my rubbery glove!'

'Oh my old love,' whispered the glove.

'I know, Father, I know,' said Sarah Jane in tears – somehow my thoughts were getting to her. They must be. 'I do know, and yet there's something in this sovereign here, something more to it. I do know it! Oh, why am I thinking of James Henry so? Why does he flood back to me, it's as if I see him now in the cupboard there where we used to hide. Why can I not get him from my head?'

'You're upsetting yourself, Sarah Jane,' said her brother, 'and you're upsetting Mother too. It isn't right. You oughtn't to.'

'I cannot let you destroy it!' cried Sarah Jane.

'Just you try and stop me, my girl!' said the father, holding long tongs now and coming forward with purpose.

'No, Father, you mustn't!' she cried and scooped me up.

And just at that moment there came a quiet knock at the door.

For the Heapsick

The family stopped dead. They looked at one another in a panic, but Sarah Jane held on to me and when the father put out his hand, she shook her head.

Another quiet knock at the door.

'Sarah Jane,' whispered the mother, 'give it over to your father. Now.'

'Hello,' called Sarah Jane, 'who is it out there? Who's at the door?'

''Tis old Percy Howlett,' came the voice beyond. 'May I step in?'

'It's only Percy,' said the grandmother. 'I've known him since I was but a girl in new leathers. Let him in, he shan't do any harm.'

'Sarah Jane,' said the father in determined whispers, 'will you give that to me this instant?'

'No, Father, I do not think that I shall,' said Sarah Jane as she opened the door. 'Dear Mr Howlett, won't you come in? So sorry to have kept you.'

'Evening all,' said an old, thin voice. 'Not disturbing anything, am I?'

The Haywards, every one of them, were quick to say not.

'Only,' said the old man, 'I heard raised voices. Did I call at the wrong time?'

'No, no, Percy, don't talk rot,' said the grandmother. 'Come now, sit by me.'

I heard shuffling and wheezing.

'Your cold's no better then, Percy?'

'No, no, not much it isn't. My dancing days are spent, I reckon. Hot in here, isn't it? Hot as hell I reckon!'

'Is it, Percy?' said the father. 'Doesn't feel so hot to me.'

'Nor me, nor me,' echoed various Haywards.

'That pan's red hot!' the old man exclaimed.

'So it is!' said the mother. 'I'd quite forgotten it. William Henry, take it off the stove.'

'What's new, Percy?'

'Fearful flap about, ain't there. Looking for sovereigns!' said the old man, laughing. 'They can search me right enough, how many sovereigns do I have upon me? Don't you hear me rattling with sovereigns? Idiots, what idiots! How many of us in Filching should have sovereigns now, I ask you. But I come this eveningtide with a tin, I'm afraid. I'm collecting for the heapsick. There's awful fever about. I know a family all dependent on their eldest son but he collapsed into a boathook Friday last and now the family sit about the unhappy object, starving. I hate to ask, but do you have anything? Anything at all?'

'Oh, Percy, we've not been doing well, you know,' said the mother.

'We have something surely,' said the grandmother. 'A ha'penny bit, surely, for Percy and his heapsick. We can manage that can't we? I shan't have it said the Haywards give nothing!'

'Go on then, Sarah Jane,' said the mother, 'give over a ha'penny, but don't call again soon Percy. We're not Iremongers you know, we're not made a money.'

'I shan't, I promise. I hate to do it.'

Sarah Jane, still holding me, fetched a coin from a cup on a shelf with her other hand and gave it over. The old man quickly clasped his withered hands over Sarah Jane's and so over me. He held on to her. I could feel Sarah Jane struggling, beginning to panic.

'Bless you child, bless you.'

'Percy, Percy Howlitt,' exclaimed the grandmother, 'is that a new umbrella you have there?'

'It is, it is,' said the old man, 'to keep the weather and me a distance from each other.'

'How ever did you afford it?'

'It was gifted to me, most generous.'

I heard the umbrella then, it was whispering, 'Barnaby Macmillan, a brolley, his brolley, would that I wasn't.'

'Well, dear Haywards,' said the old man, 'I must be on now, I've my tin to rattle elsewhere alas, and it does feel to me fearsome warm in here.'

'What's the rush, Percy? Have a bite with us.'

'No, thank you, thank you, I must on, really I must.'

'It's not like you to turn down a meal. You're skin and bones, Percy, come now, take a bite. When did you last eat? I won't have it said the Haywards are a mean people.'

'No, no, honest, I must get on. Please detain me no further.'

'Don't be rude, Percy, it doesn't suit.'

'Please stay, Percy, you've got to eat.'

'No!' the old man shrieked. 'I've got to get on! Urgent!'

'Why, Percy Howlett, what a way to behave, how cruel you are.'

'You're not yourself, Percy, to snap at us so.'

The old man was panting and rushing about in the room.

'Well, well,' the old man gasped at last, 'the truth is, I can't keep food in me. It won't stay down.'

'Oh, Percy, poor dear man, have some grinding will you then, have some physic. Smoke a pipe.'

'Thankee, thankee, dear friends,' the old man wheezed, 'but I've already had some, thankee kindly. I've just been to chemist Griggs and he set me up.'

'What Griggs have you, Percy? When was that?'

'Just five minutes ago.'

'Five minutes ago you were at Griggses?'

'Yes indeed, just a few moments before seeing you, he set me up.'

'Well goodnight then, Percy,' said the father, 'mind how you go.'

'Goodnight, all!'

The door was closed, the family silent a moment and then,

'Why did the old man lie to us, why did he say that?'

'Something's up, Herbert Arthur,' said the mother. 'I don't like it.'

'To think I've known him since I was a girl,' said the grandmother, 'and have trusted him all these years.'

'We must get it out! We must get it out quick. We have to lose it!'

'Sarah Jane! Sarah Jane! Where are you going!'

'Come back! Come back!'

But Sarah Jane was already out the door, still holding me tight, out the door and running.

Under the Bridge

Sarah Jane was running, running, running for all her life.

'Stop! Stop there!' someone called out.

But Sarah Jane didn't stop, she rushed on. There was a whistle blown somewhere behind us. On she ran, on and on. She stopped suddenly, I could just see through her fingers a man before us with a wooden barrel. He had a rag covering over his face. He was pouring whatever was in the barrel down a coal chute, into an old house. He looked about, most perturbed.

'Who are you?' asked Sarah Jane.

But the man stopped, he looked at her a moment, such a cleanliness about him, as if he was not a Foulsham creature at all.

'Who are you?' she asked again. 'You're not from here are you?'

The whistle sounded again, the clean man ran off into the darkness, and Sarah Jane ran too, in a different direction. She slid a little, but was up again. Noises of people behind us. She slowed at last. She stopped. She was panting so. We were crouched down under a bridge of some sort. There was an upturned bucket down there, dented, with a brass ring about its handle. Sarah Jane knocked it over, it rolled under the bridge.

'I think we're safe, safe here a while.'

She brought me up to her eyes.

'There you are then,' she said. 'I wonder if you're not James Henry, I think you might be. Oh, you're definitely someone, I know you are. Are you James Henry, are you? To think at last you come home and we nearly murder you. I'll keep you safe, James Henry. I'll hide you somewhere, yes, that's it! Somewhere that no one can ever find you, but somewhere where I can still get to you. But where is that? Where is that place? Who's there?' She suddenly stood up. 'Who is it?'

There was a movement in the shadows beneath the bridge. From the darkness a rat scuttled forwards. It did not run from a human in fear but rather sauntered closely, as if we were disturbing it and it had a mind to tell us off.

'Oh, a rat,' said Sarah Jane, 'only a rat. You gave me quite a scare. I'd trap you, you're huge. We'd get a good price for you. Go on now, get out of it, before I put an end on you with my boot. Get on! Get out!'

But the rat, rather than rushing away, sat down now, scratched its face with a forepaw, and just stayed there, looking up at Sarah Jane.

'Go on!' she cried. 'Get!'

But the rat sat on.

'Go! Get away!'

The rat's head moved a little to the side, as if it were purposefully looking at Sarah Jane from a new angle.

'I said *get*!' She was up now, and stepped towards it.

But the rat stayed where it was, looking at her. Then it hissed.

'You great bully, you foul filthy thing! I hate you! I'm going to squash you under my boot!'

The rat hissed.

'You don't frighten me,' she said. 'I'm not going to be frightened by some rat. My family have killed rats for generations, that's what we do, we Haywards. We've a license for it. I know rats, I know what they look like inside and out. I've skinned hundreds on them. I've a mind to make you into part of a hat. I'll use your tail to tie up my boots. I'll boil your bones up for glue, see if I don't.'

Hiss, went the rat.

'I'm going to pop out your eyes, I am. I'm going to hear your bones snap!'

Hiss, went the rat.

'You're dead, rat! You are dead!'

Hiss, went the rat.

'What's that on you, rat? An old ring, quite caught round your waist, you dirt thing, you, I'll catch you!'

I listened out. I heard the big brass ring. It barely murmured, 'Agatha Peel.'

'Hiss!'

'Come on then! Come on!'

Hiss, went the rat.

Hiss, went the rat, and then it lunged.

'Ow!' cried Sarah Jane, for the rodent had bit into her hand, and she had dropped me upon the ground. 'You, rat, you shall pay for that! I'm cut! I'm bleeding!'

The rat was running about on the floor, sniffing at me dreadfully.

'Where's it gone, where's my sov?'

The body around me seemed to grow larger of a sudden.

'What are you? You're a cat! You weren't a cat afore! How did you do that?'

What only a moment ago had been a rat was now a large, fat, scarred, bristling, hissing tortoiseshell cat, rabid with disease, fleas and flies thick about it. The old brass ring, Agatha Peel, fixed high upon one leg.

'Give it back! Give it back!'

The cat hissed. It dropped its whole body over me, and I could see nothing.

'I'll have it, I'll have it now! Get gone you filthy beast!'

It hissed, it screamed; how it screamed, an awful human scream.

And Sarah Jane was stumbling.

'You're not natural!' screamed Sarah Jane.

The foul cat screeched to make your blood freeze over.

And Sarah Jane slipped on the ground as she tried to kick the thing, but the foul cat was rushing towards her, on the attack.

Help! Oh help her!

There was a frightful bellow then and the cat went flying. Someone else had kicked the beast, someone else was there. Who was it? Someone tall, some thin new figure, in a dark coat.

'You know me, girl,' he said.

'No,' she said, her face white in terror, 'I never . . .'

'You *do* know me.'

'I know you,' trembled Sarah Jane. 'Oh, please, please! Don't murder me! HELP!'

'Rrrrrun!' said the terrible emaciated man. 'While you're still able!'

That got her shifting, screaming for all she was able, poor Sarah Jane scrabbled up and was away from the bridge and screaming yet.

The cat shrieked, and was very suddenly a seagull, a grim looking piece, a very red tip to its beak.

'Ark!' it screamed.

'Come here, Feathers. I need to unbutton you.'

'Ark! Ark!' it screamed and up it went, labouring hard to climb high, screaming all the while, 'Ark, ark!' A warning, it was screaming a warning, this creature, a call, an alert.

The thin man picked me up from the dirt, wiped me off. 'What have we here?'

He held a pair of scissors, pinking shears they were.

The Tailor, here was the Tailor.

And then came the pain.

7

THE HEAPS ARE KNOCKING

Continuing the narrative of Lucy Pennant

Acid. Acid inside me. Burning. Like someone had lit a fire. Like I was on fire, burning up, that I'd be no more than a mound of ash in a second. Don't know how long it went on like that, the pain something terrible. I was drowning in it, couldn't do anything but hurt. I wondered if I was dying, if that was what it felt like. I wondered if this was the end of it, that I should die here, deep in the darkness with this cruel abused thing beside me. No doubt he'd eat me. What a way to end it.

But I didn't die, not yet, not then anyways.

I was dark under the pain, suffocated by it, and there were terrible dreams about buttons and clay and I thought I should be a clay thing, baked of mud, in the earth where it's all dark and cold. But I was fighting it, striking back, biting my own illness. Clawing at it. I shall not be a button. I shall not do it, get off me. Dreams of matches striking me, of being buried in a box of matches and a thin strict woman with a veil over her face, looking at me straight and saying, 'Me! Me! Me!'

'Me! Me! Me!' I called back, and as I called back I came back, back, back to me, I'd fought the thing off.

'Binadit.'

I was back there in the dark deep. The thing, Benedict I must call him, was beside me. Couldn't see him, just heard him, and, Lord knows, smelt the fellow.

'Binadit.'

'Get away!' I cried, kicking out. 'Get away from me!'

'Binadit,' he said, but further away.

'Were you trying to eat me, Benedict, were you?'

'Hongry.'

'Don't you dare.'

'Hongry?'

'I'm not on the menu!'

'No! Hongry?'

'Do you mean, am *I* hungry? Are you trying to feed me?'

'Have fed you, you've been sickening, I've been feeding and drinking. Went up. Got new! You ate, you ate it all.'

'You've been feeding me?'

'Yes, yes, Binadit! I thought you'd be a botton. I thought you might. I wanted a botton, but you said you'd get me more bottons. So then get me, get me.'

'How long have I been ill?'

'Long?'

'How many hours, or days?'

'No day down here. No clocks. I went up twice, light the first, dark the second. Space inbetween. Your skin was getting stiff, you started getting small, but I shouted at you and you come back big again.'

'I think I must thank you, Benedict. I think I must, I'm being fought. There's someone somewhere who has been made a box of matches and I don't think she likes it. She's fighting me, Benedict, she'll keep fighting me. She's quiet now, she's just matches now somewhere, but she's still thinking. I know it. She's gathering her strength; she longs to be human again.'

'Don't let her!'

'She's tough, I felt her. She so wants to live.'

'I want my bottons!'

'And you shall have them. You have earnt them all right.'

'Like bottons. Do like bottons.'

'Benedict, is there any light? I think a little light might help me.'

'No, no, no more light, all light spent.'

'I need light. Can we go up? I want to go up. I must get out!'

The fear of being trapped down in the darkness was too great for me. I felt all the heaps breathing all about me. I felt so lost deep within it, that I was drowning, drowning.

'Get me out of here!'

'Do you hurt? Is it the match woman coming for you?'

'No, no, it's the heaps. The feel of them, the weight of them!'

'Don't fight it. Mustn't.'

'Please, I must get out!'

'It'll know if you're frightened. It'll know it. It'll come for you if you're frightened. It'll get you.'

'Please, please, which way? I must have light!'

'No, no! Lucy Pennant, listen.'

'Help me! Help me, please!'

'You'll crush us. It won't let us be if you hate it!'

Just then there was a fearsome smash against the metal walls of Benedict's hovel, things knocking against it from the outside, things scraping against the metal walls, making terrible screeching, screaming noises.

'It heard you,' said Benedict. 'It heard your fear and now is come.'

'We have to get out! Right now!'

'No, no, mustn't. Can't go now. 'Tisn't safe. Must stay.'

'I can't stay! I'm suffocating!'

'Binadit, Binadit,' he said quietly, stroking my hair.

'Don't touch me!'

'You're frightened, not to be, not to be.'

The noise of things smacking and shifting against the metal room grew louder and louder, a drumming against the walls, huge things trying to crush us.

'We're going to die! I'm going to die here.'

'No, no, we're not.'

'Help me!'

'Trying to help you. Am trying.'

'What then . . . What was that? Oh God!' Something was drilling against the walls, the whole room was shuddering, then the boom, boom, boom, we were shaken in our cage, our vault, our trap, our tomb. 'Tell me, oh please tell me. What will make it stop?'

'You must be stiller, you must not be scared. It knows you're scared, and that's what scared it, and when it gets scared it gets fretful and then it pounds and crushes and is a big terrible thing. So, so, Lucy Pennant, not to frighten it.'

'I frighten it?'

'You do,' he shouted above the noise of all those things come to crush us. 'Tell me, Lucy Pennant, a nice story. Tell me a story of Lucy Pennant, so to keep us all calm and put away the storming.'

And so, gasping and shaking, I stammered out the story of my childhood, of the boarding house where I lived, of Father and of Mother, of running up and down that house, of finding things, of stealing a bit here and there, of looking in on the homes of all those different people, and of the man upstairs at the top of the house whose door was always closed, who never came out at all, but we could hear him, me and my friends, moving about inside. I told all of Filching, and of the orphanage and of the red-haired girl Mary Staggs and of coming to Heap House, and of being a serving girl, and of Clod, of my Clod and his plug and of kissing him, and of promising him, no matter what, that I should find him again.

When I had finished it was a shock to learn that all was calm, that nothing was tapping against the walls, the storm in the deeps had stopped. I was not frightened and, now I must believe, it, the great thing beyond, was not frightened either.

'Lucy Pennant,' said Benedict quietly, 'she has talked to the Heaps, and they have listened.'

And I said, smiling, despite of all, because I could but help it, and it seemed the only possible way to mark the occasion, 'Binadit!'

We stayed in the darkness, listening to the heaps growing

111

quieter. The tapping on the walls ever less frequent and fainter.

'Is it going away?' I asked.

'It is always here, it don't ever go,' said Benedict, 'but sometime it is angry and sometime it is not. Not now. Calm now. What a thing it is!'

'Is it safe to go up?'

'Safe for me.'

'I must get out, I cannot stay here.'

Something banged against the walls.

'It hears you,' he said.

'I don't mind it,' I said. 'It may do as it pleases, but I shall not stay in here the rest of my days. I mean to go out and I mean for it to let me. It bloody shall.'

I listened then, listened for its banging, but no sound came.

'Will it let me go?' I asked.

'Is your decision,' said Benedict. 'Is for you to be calm and unfrit.'

'Well then, I am,' I said. 'Well then let us go, I must find Clod. He'll be waiting for me. He won't be able to do anything without me. Never could, the booby. I quite miss him. Ow!'

My leg hurt so when I moved it, as if it had been crushed, as if a part of it had been torn off, and there was a crust of blood there, a scab.

'When you was sleeping,' he said, 'of a sudden your leg was bleeding. Wasn't me that done, it just sprung a leak, most strange.'

'All on its own.'

'Yes, yes, of its own.'

'Benedict,' I said, 'you help me and I'll help you. What do

I want: to get out of here and to find Clod and to stop that woman of matches. What do you want: buttons. Very good then, I'll show you to buttons. We'll go into Filching for buttons, oh they have buttons there.'

'Filching?'

'That's right, is it far?'

'Depends on the weather. Up to the Heaps.'

'Well, Benedict, the sooner we start the sooner we arrive. I'll find my friends there, and I'll gather my strength up. Yes, that's it. In Filching I'll work out just what to do.'

'They put you in a cage there and show you off to crowds. They gives you all sorts to eat and they beat you and laugh at you. That's Filchin'.'

'They did that to you?'

'Big crowds! All looking in at me. I was in a cage! Different, they says a me, so different you are, as always, not actually a mun, nor either a thing. Want to be wanted. Want to be! Don't want to be in a cage. Things not mun, things it was that chose me, welcomed me. Free now, free to run and eat as I likes!'

'Over in Filching I've friends, Benedict, and they shall be your friends too.'

'I was born out in the Heaps, Heaps is my home. I'd be all at sea anyplace other.'

'Will you help me, Benedict?'

'It's not Benedict, it's Binadit. That's my proper name. That or It, they called me. Binadit, Binadit!'

'Steady now, Benedict, don't get so excited.'

'Binadit! Is Binadit to call!'

'What sort of a name is that, Binadit? I shall call you Benedict, which at least is a proper name.'

'Binadit, is Binadit!'

'We'll see.'

'I'll eat you.'

'No, no, you shan't. We will need money.'

'Money!' spat Benedict. 'Have money!'

Benedict rattled around in one of his dirty cupboards and came out clinking all about him, and rustling. Coins, coins and even paper money. How much finding in the heaps he had done himself, how much he'd kept away from the Iremonger sorters. He was a rich man living in squalor.

'Well!' I cried, feeling all them notes. 'Behold the Bank of England!'

'You laugh at me! Don't like it!'

'Happily, Benedict, you're a rich fellow from what I feel all about us, you're rolling in it. What a person you are!'

'Am I?'

'Yes,' I said, 'yes, I truly think you are.'

He grunted at that, I think it was a happy grunt.

'Well then, Benedict, gather up your money and let us go up to the surface and into Filching.'

'Up? It's not up for Filchin'. Is down, down for Filchin', along the pipes, get in the pipes, go along, bit wet as maybe, but is the quickest way. No, it's down, down is best for Filchin'. Sometimes I sit there, on the edge, and watch them, watch them people peopling. No, no, down, must down for Filch.'

'What pipes, Benedict?'

'Them pipes, the tunnel. The Effra!'

'What's the Effra?'

'Don't know?'

'Never heard of.'

''Tis the lost river, the Effra is! Was once on ground in Roman days they told me, now under the ground. Still flows the Effra does, but underneath, been bricked over and used now much for swidge and such, under it is, flowing still. Is still alive, only buried, still flowing, only out of sight. Flows all the way to the Thames it does, so they says. I ain't never seen the Thames.'

'Well then, Benedict, let us find this lost river.'

'And catch a lift on it. It'll take us, the Effra will.'

8

TO BREATHE AGAIN

Continuing the narrative of Clod Iremonger

I Fall Out to Myself

The emaciated man picked me up from the dirt, scissors in his hands.

A seagull cried overhead, 'Ark! Ark!'

Then the pain came, like I was splitting and shifting inside, like I should rupture myself.

'Not yet, mustn't yet,' the Tailor hissed. 'It's too open, keep small, you devil! It's not safe!'

But I was struggling and shifting, hurting so, I couldn't calm, wouldn't calm, I should burst.

'Curse you!' he cried.

Then, holding me hard in his fist, he ran. For a while I was only aware of moving fast and turning, dashing, onwards and onwards, and then we would stop suddenly, wait a moment, and then on, sometimes I heard cries behind us, then he hastened on further and faster. He hid in the entryway to a house, stood in the shadows, panting in a porch. People rushed by, people with lanterns, and some pushing some sort of wheelbarrow, and in that wheelbarrow, I heard a voice that I was shocked to understand I knew, because behind it a metal instrument sounded its sharp noise,

'Geraldine Whitehead.'

'Wait, wait, hold you there my lovelies!' My Uncle Idwid, the Governor of Birth Objects, was very close to me, listening in the street, his ears out on high alert. 'I hear something, silence all. Not a sound. Hush, hush. I do hear! Come now, a little louder, a little more yet. I'm certain I heard.

'Come to me, oh come, come to me. Don't be shy now. It is your own uncle calling. You can hear me. I know you can. You are in terrible danger. Let me help you. Just whisper, whisper your name. Let me hear that little syllable: Clod. Come, Clod. Come, come, Clod to me, sing Clod to me.'

All the people were still around him as the little man in the wheelbarrow listened out. The Tailor pushed me deep down in his pocket, and I in my agony tried so hard to think of nothing, I tried to be nothing, nothing at all, to forget the pain.

'I heard 'Iremonger'! I heard at least one thing call 'Iremonger!' Where are you, love? Speak to me!'

Silence. Silence but the distant noise of the heaps and the drip dripping of Foulsham Town.

'You're here. I know you're here somewhere!' sang Uncle Idwid. 'I can almost hear you. Whisper, just whisper and I'll come to thee.'

Such an itching, such an agony to call out, to scream out my name, as if Idwid in all his cleverness was tickling me with his words.

'You've grown strong. You've grown cunning, little Clod, but you cannot hide from me. You cannot fool such ears as mine. I can hear you, I can hear your very soul, Clod, I hear it breathing!'

And I should have screamed, I should have called out there and then and surrendered myself to the sharpness of Geraldine Whitehead were it not for the sudden noise of heavy boots breaking the irresistible call of Idwid's will.

'Idiot!' he cried. 'I should have had him but for thee! Manlump, thick of ears, deaf of mind! Fool, noise-murderer!'

'Please sir, please governor!'

'What, what is it, you thug?'

'There's been a half sovereign spotted, sir. In a ratcatcher's house!'

'All the cacophony of Foulsham streets: it's enough to make a fellow mad. Who saw the coin? When?'

'There's a man over yonder, sir, under that umbrella there. He's the one that saw it, swears he did.'

'Well then, that's different, we may hear *him* a little.'

The whole brood, noisy now, rushed away, and I felt at last I might breathe a little. In a moment the Tailor was on the move too, putting streets between him and Uncle Idwid's party. But there were watchmen everywhere; it seemed from every corner I heard voices calling out.

'Not yet, not yet!' he said. He took me out, held me in his hands, nearly dropped me. 'So hot! We shall not make it back in time. Curse you. We must do it here; we must find a place!'

He ran on for a while longer, stopped in somewhere and, with the aid of a handkerchief, he placed me on the ground. The Tailor was looming over me. I saw him clear then for the first time. He was a very tall, shabbily dressed man in a long coat of patched leathers, unhappily tall, like he'd been pulled and stretched, with a white, livid face, with eyebrows that joined in the centre, very lean and underfed almost to the point of being a skeleton. He swallowed; he looked at me.

'You have caused much trouble this night!'

He came close and tapped me with one of his emaciated fingers.

'I shall not hang for thee!'

He pulled at his own lank black hair.

'I shall not be put out on account of you,' he cried. 'But come now, come! Will you not come out, you're hot enough. Come, before it is too light and we are trapped here. It must be now. Now! Come out!'

And then –

And then –

And then.

The pain! The burning pain.

And then, breathing, breathing as if I'd never breathed before. How my arms seemed to tug from me, my legs to rip out of me, my head, my boiling brain seemed to bubble up in agony. Spreading out, filling up, back, back.

Alive.

There I was.

Clod.

I was me again. I was flesh once more.

Flesh again in some dingy, abandoned place.

And I said the only words I could at first say,

'Clod Iremonger, Clod Iremonger, Clod Iremonger!'

'Shut it! Shut it, Clod Iremonger,' said the Tailor, 'or you'll have the whole town down upon me. Shut it, or you'll give us all away.'

'Clod,' I whispered.

'Careful,' he said, raising a fist.

'Iremonger,' I involuntarily finished.

'Not a sound, Clod Iremonger,' he said, his long scissors in his hands now, 'or they'll hear you. Not a murmur. There's someone in the alley. Another squeak and I swear I'll gut you here and now.'

Binadit

9

THE EFFRA AND AFTER

Continuing the narrative of Lucy Pennant

I cannot say what it was that we passed through in the darkness, only sometimes it cut me and sometimes it wetted me, sometimes it moved as I touched it. Once it bit, once it was soft and even warm, and all of it passed alongside me as Benedict, pulling on a length of rope he had tied about my waist, pulled me down and down after him.

You don't feel you're falling so much if there are objects all around you, pressing against you, trying not to let you have your bit of space. Down through his little passages, moving bits before me out of the way, and when I was stuck he did not try to carefully win my freedom. His answer was only to tug me down and down by force, to muscle the objects out of the way. There are holes in the heaps, deep lanes, tunnels like the flues of the chimneys of Heap House and like them with hot and cold breaths, and with other creatures, rats as big as cats, forcing their own way along them, unhappy at the company.

At last we came to the bottom, or rather to a shelf in all that rotting land. I tried to call to him but there was no sound to come out of you that deep, and breathing was the hardest thing all on its own, the air so thick and soiled it felt liquid.

We forced our way along on top of a huge brick ceiling. At last there was some kind of hatch, for which Benedict found the thick cover and lifted it up and he pushed me through first and there were winding stone steps but no light, and the going was very wet and I slipped and soon enough the steps came to an end and there was only the sound of water then, rushing by.

'What now?' I asked. 'There's no more steps.'

'Jump,' he said.

'How far is it?' I asked. 'Stop, Benedict, I'll fall to my death I think.'

In response he shoved me and I fell in and he came after.

Icy, icy water. Quite took my breath from me.

We were in the buried river called the Effra, being swept along. I thought I should freeze to death. I'd be ice any moment. The place was alive with dripping sounds, with the plonk, plonk, of water dropping down, and then of waves, of things moving in the dark flow. Like being inside the organs of a massive whale, swimming along its colon.

'Is low tide,' he said.

'What luck,' I panted. The river was slowing and I could stand now, shivering and miserable, the foulness reaching quite up to my waist.

What a place it was, long ago, so long ago ancient Britons must have fished this river, and Romans had marched beside it, where I was now. Only then, back then, back then the river was on the surface, there'd be ground and sunlight beside us. The past, our past is buried deep beneath us, dig down and there is ancient land. Alfred the Great might have bathed where we waded.

'And here's our stopping,' called Benedict. 'Here's Filchin' steps now.'

He could see in the damp darkness, I could not. He had us winding up different slipping steps, not so many, and after a moment Benedict had found the manhole cover, and there was a circle of light.

Filching!

It was early evening. The sky was darkening which was never best bright in Filching, but bright brightness did it seem after that dank darkness. Like I was newly bathed in life, more beautiful than I ever knew possible.

'Filchin' foul,' said Benedict. 'I know the smell on it.'

'You showed me the way back there in those different darks, now I'll show you. I'll be your candle, Benedict, allow me.'

I saw him properly then, in Filching light. To think I'd taken up with such a one as that. You're braver that I thought, Lucy Pennant. He really did not seem a human being exactly, more a great mound of rubbish joined together into something almost human-shaped. There were eyes but they were so dark and yellowed they were hard to notice. The mouth more a rip than anything else. The hair was a wiry threadbare growth of weed. The clothing he wore was not to be described in any way like other people wore clothes, no recognisable garments there, just different things grown together. Bits of rat stuck upon him like fur in patches. If he wasn't moving you'd take him for just a pile of stuff, not living, just raked up. Like a mountain all of his own. But this, even this, was a person, this giant beside me.

'Don't like it,' he said, and he had begun a-trembling. 'Don't like it here. Don't want no cage.'

'It's all right, Benedict. I promise you.'

'You got no power to promise. Who are you to promise anything? You don't know, you're as nothing. You're a little bit with a bright red top. What protection can that be? No, no I shan't. Go home!'

'But what is home, Benedict? What is there for you? It's just rubbish and filth. I shall show you new things, new things and new people. You'll find a home here, here among the lodgings of Filching.'

We had come out close to the heap wall, it was very cracked the wall was, it never used to be so cracked, there were metal girders propping it up and huge buttresses made of brick. I wondered how long it should hold. I thought then it surely shall come down one day.

In the distance I saw the long slipway leading up to the wall. It was lined thick with carts piled high with London dirt. There were carts back as far as the eye could see, a great queue of wastedroppers. It was always so, it was a familiar enough sight. The carts came and went with their heavy loads through the day and into the night. They never stopped coming, there never was an end on it. More and more and more. Seagulls were thick about it all and on the other side, I knew, there would be a whole great army of Filching sorters, all of them married to the heaps, thousands of them, with their forks and pikes and shovels and bags, and the rats working their own work between them.

Has always been so. Would seem most strange for that road to have no carts on it, not to see the full ones lining up, not to see the empty ones going back. The horses pulled the loads and were whipped to keep them at it. They pulled and were pulled, until, giving up, buckling under the hopeless endlessness of it all, they slumped to the ground, were opened up and skinned on the spot, or if there were already too many gulls and rats about the carcass, they were shovelled over the wall and into it with all the rest. It was a grand and harrowing sight. Something Bible about it all.

'My home,' I said. 'Here I am.'

Binadit grunted.

'Well then,' I said, my teeth chattering, my whole body shaking with the cold. 'We'd best get in before we freeze to death.'

'Am fearful.'

'No need.'

'Your hair,' he said.

'What of it?'

'Most red.'

'Yes,' I said, 'always has been. Can't help it.'

'Like it,' he said. 'Fond on it.'

'I'm going home,' I said. 'I'm going to where I grew up, to where I lived with Mother and Father before they got the sickness and died. I'm going back there, to my old boarding house!'

'On then,' he said, grinning I think, I couldn't be sure. 'Show us! Bottons!'

'Here we go!'

'Lucy Pennant,' he said and the clarity of it was a bit alarming, 'don't be a botton. Stay as now ever.'

'I'll do my best,' I said. 'Come on!'

Alexander Erkmann,
The Tailor of Foulsham

10

THE TAILOR OF FOULSHAM

Continuing the narrative of Clod Iremonger

My Companion

'Clod Iremonger,' I said, though I'd rather have said something else. 'Help' should be more justified. 'Help', screamed out, may have been the most sensible.

In response the long jaws of his scissors snapped once. And came closer, and snapped again.

I think I should rather have been any place, than in a mean hovel with a man so lean and stretched. I think I may rather have been back with the Hayward family, or even with the coins of the pieshop. But I was in this dismal, dark place, hopeless and lightless, abandoned by all other people, fit for nothing, fit for no person, for no thing. How was it that I felt less free now than I did when coined. I was myself, but how long may I stay so?

'Clod,' I whispered, 'Iremonger?'

'Yes,' said the Tailor and the scissors snapped once to his syllable, he leant in very close to me. I saw then that his very skeleton was stretched and thinned out, that his own skull beneath the limited pelt of his horrible skin was most elongated. 'Yes, you are Clod Iremonger,' he whispered. 'Do you know me, Iremonger? Do you remember me?'

'Clo— no, sir,' I managed now. 'I think I should recall you if ever we had met before. You are rather singular, sir. I mean no offence, but, excuse me sir, are you quite well?'

'You do not know me?'

'Please to excuse, I've not been myself of late, which brings me to wonder, sir, if you yourself were not exactly as you are now. That you have, perchance, over the time since our last acquaintance, if indeed there were ever such a thing, if you might have – a suggestion only, you understand – have added some to your height while perhaps simultaneously mislaying a fraction of your width?'

How I cursed myself. No matter how I struggled against it, whenever I was in position of worry and terror I come over with a fit of talkativeness, and spouted out and could not stop myself from filling the room, perhaps in the hope of taking away a portion of the fear with words. Tummis, my dear late cousin, was much the same. And this was perhaps one of the causes of our intimacy.

'You wonder if I have changed?' he said, his painful face come close again.

'Am I very much mistook?' I said, though I'd hoped to make a simple 'yes'.

'Indeed, Clod Iremonger, I am changed, indeed I am. Last you saw me, I was but nine inches long!'

'Then indeed, sir, you have made quite a progress! Indeed you have!'

The Tailor pulled from a deep pocket a bundle wrapped in thick cloth, he unravelled the material to reveal a very dented and abused hip flask. 'Recognise this?' he asked.

I had never seen the object before and was about to admit as much but then I heard its particular noise, a strained, shrunken calling out.

'Rippit Iremonger, Rippit Iremonger!'

And then I listened and heard within that stretched, bony form of the Tailor the sound leaking out, 'Letter opener. Letter opener.'

'Excuse me sir, but would it be relevant for me to wonder if that is not my cousin Rippit who was taken from us so many years ago?'

'Very like, Clod Iremonger, very like. Though how you know so quick, I cannot say.'

'And, excuse me then, sir, if I may wonder, is your name, your real name, might it be, Alexander Erkmann?'

'Why yes, you devil!'

My Cousin Rippit, Now a Hip Flask

'I do remember Cousin Rippit,' I said.

There was never any forgetting of my cousin Rippit. Cousin Rippit had been Grandfather's favourite. Dangerous Cousin

Rippit who could set someone's hair alight just for the fun of it, just by thinking of it. Cousin Rippit who bent metal just by pointing at it. Cousin Rippit whose calls of pain in the night upset the whole house.

He was always ill, was Cousin Rippit, ill and dangerous. You might try to help him, you'd put your hand out to help him, and suddenly your hand would grow numb and have blisters upon it, because Rippit had somehow bewitched it. We steered clear of Rippit, we younger cousins, and I think the older ones too, and because of that he had a look of terrible loneliness about him, even as he was being cruel.

I did not know him very well. Once he attempted to drop a book on my head from a great height, he nearly brained me. Once he got hold of one Tummis's seagulls and plucked it without killing it. It was a very unhappy thing, that naked bird, until the rats got to it. And then, one day, he was gone, and later, much later, on that terrible evening when Lucy fell before me into a button, Grandfather told me that Rippit, most gifted and strangest of all Iremongers, had been subdued and stolen by his own birth object, a letter opener that I had heard calling 'Alexander Erkmann'. And here was Alexander Erkmann in the flesh, my companion in this cruel shed.

'He doesn't like to be made so small,' said the Tailor. 'How he struggles and twists himself over it. We've so stretched and pulled and hurt the shape of each other, we've corrupted and deformed ourselves. We're bent out of all order and shall not come back right again.'

'Poor Cousin Rippit!'

'You see how we have changed over these five years, how I

have stretched and tugged and how he has shrunk and dented and rusted. How we have hurt one another. I am not as strong as once I was and sometimes, particularly of late, I fear he may get the better of me. But he has not yet, though he pulls me so hard!' The Tailor wrapped and returned the flask to his pocket. 'Back at Heap House, your cousin had a certain way with objects. He summoned up people every now and then, pulled them briefly from the objects they had become. He stalked the house upsetting things, bullying them, bringing them for the briefest moments back to themselves, only for them to be drowned once more back into object form. There was pain all over the House, the things were hurting.'

'Yes, there is truth in this. The objects do hurt so!'

'One day your cousin called upon the object nearest him, to bring it out, just for a moment he hoped, and then to close it back in the form of a letter opener knife. Thus did I stretch and stand once more, and thus did I pounce and keep him there, that twisted metal soul: your cousin the hip flask!'

'Poor Cousin, though he was never kind to me, still I say it, poor Cousin.'

'Rippit Iremonger,' said the abused metal from deep within the pocket.

'Begging your pardon, sir,' I said, 'but what shall you do to me? Shall you tailor me?'

'I have been tracking you, Clod Iremonger. I have read the bill posters, seen the policing doubled, seen the Iremongers come out from their gates because of you. That's not normal, that's not like them. They keep their distance in general, from all the filth. I've been after you since I understood how much they wanted you. I told myself, if they want you so much, then *I* should be the one to have you. Why are they after you, Clod Iremonger, why do they want you so?'

'I cannot say, sir.'

'Well they shall have you again, true enough, once I have emptied you out. Once you shall cause no harm.'

'I do no harm, sir. I do not indeed.'

'Listen to me, Clod Iremonger, listen well – ever since I stole to Foulsham I've had but one purpose in my life, one solid purpose that never have I stirred from though it stretch me and pull me so I snap. I do not waver, it gives me reason. My life: to go about me in these foul streets and to poke at Iremongers with something sharp, to find me some lonely Iremonger down a lonely street and to send him off, as his kind has to so many others. But rarely, no I shall admit it, *never* have I had a full Iremonger in my reaching. I am Revenge, Clod Iremonger. That is my title!'

'You won't hurt me, shall you, sir, Mr Erkmann?'

'Shan't I? I think I might.'

'Please not to. I never hurt anyone so much as ever I was aware of.'

'Your name is enough hurt right there, your name's done a thousand, thousand murderings!'

'I cannot help my name!'

'No more can I,' said he, lifting the scissors above his head. 'Say your prayers now.'

I closed my eyes. I waited for the sharpness to come.

In the hovel I heard the sounds of things calling out in darkness. I had not heard them before, but now as I concentrated the voices declared themselves loudly.

'Elsa Howard, now a nail.'

'Horace Bentley, wooden plank.'

'Wilfred Pilcher, under the straw, a child's left glove long forgot.'

'Mr Sandford, a pillow cover, rag now.'

'Hello, hello to you all, I hear you,' I whispered.

'What's that?' cried the Tailor. 'Who do you talk to? Be quiet, shall you!'

'He hears us!' the things cried.'He hears us well!'

'Goodbye, dear things, goodbye to you all,' I whispered.

'Who are you talking to, Clod Iremonger? There's no one there. You and your family were ever such mad ones. But not for long I do swear it!'

'He says goodbye,' said the pillow case. 'Do you hark at that? He thinks of us before he dies. Shall we let it happen, shall we allow it?'

Their voices were a comfort to me.

'I seem to hear you all,' I said, 'in the darkness there. Can you, do you think, can you come forward perhaps? I should so like to see you now.'

It was the pain of it, the horror of my place. It must surely have been that that did it, because as I stood there now so close to my own ending, I saw Grandfather in all his high misery, moving the things about. If only I could do that, I thought, if only ever I could.

Why not? I thought. Why not, after all you're an Iremonger, you are.

'I should like, I should so like you, Wilfred,' I whispered, 'if you may, should you jump into a mouth for me?'

'Yes, sir, I think I shall, if you wish it true.'

'Elsa? Elsa, are you there still?'

'Oh, he calls my name! He calls it!'

'Elsa!' I whispered in my mounting excitement. 'Elsa, have at a hand now, shall you strike a hand that holds some scissors?'

'Stop this!' said the Tailor. 'Enough of your talking! Keep still shall you?'

'Oh, for the life of it, I shall!' called Elsa.

'And Horace, Horace, shall you strike a back?'

'I shall, with all my love!'

'Mr Sandford, I shall need you. I shall be wanting you most particular!'

'Here, I am! What service? Give the word!'

'Mr Sandford, cover a head shall you?'

'Sir, sir! Sandford's the man!'

'Now, all,' I said, 'now should be best. He comes on so close to me!'

'Now, Clod Iremonger,' called the Tailor.

Movement in the hay, sudden rustling and shifting, *things* with life and purpose, all at the rush. The Tailor turned around in a terror himself now, his scissors snapping uselessly in the dark. The nail rushed up and cut at the hand that held the scissors and the scissors dropped to the floor, the Tailor made a yelp. The plank lifted up then and struck the back, the Tailor cried out. The moment his mouth opened the glove filled the mouth, then came the pillow case over the head. And so! And so the Tailor was on the floor! In the dirt. And I stood over him.

How had I? How had I done it? I'd knocked the Tailor down,

unscissored him and had him in the dirt.

'I'm Clod Iremonger,' I said.

The Tailor made a muffled cry from beneath Mr Sandford.

'I'm Clod Iremonger,' I said, 'and I can do such things. I am Clod Iremonger, the friend of things!'

The Governor Extraordinary
of Birth Objects
Idwid Iremonger

II

IN FOULSHAM STREETS

Continuing the narrative of Lucy Pennant

We scrambled down the hill into town. It felt different to me, how to say exactly? It felt darker and damper. There was black smoke around the town that I couldn't remember being there before. It seemed to stick, that dark smoke, like it was permanent weather. The walls too, was it my imagination or did they seem to drip now? Everything was dank. Yes, it dripped, Filching Town did, never stopped dripping though there was no rain. The streets were thick with mud and waste, that was always true, but it was harder going than I recall, like we was wading back in that river again. Benedict shook a little, he trembled to be out there among the old houses, at each distant figure moving through the filthy streets he stiffened and seemed about to flee, and had often to be encouraged on.

Round a corner we surprised two men moving a great barrel. Their faces covered by rags, they were tying the barrel hard to a building. Seeing us they ran off. Something wrong about that. What was that about? But I soon enough forgot them, because there before us was clothes for the picking, clothes to warm and change us.

People as often kept their heap leathers outside as in, on account of the stench of them, especially if the weather had been rough. I grabbed at some sorry looking forms, they were hanging up on a line, trying to run away with the wind it looked like, the smoke and wind of Filching getting up the trouser legs and down the arms so that the abused leathers seemed to live by the weather. I caught up a couple and tugged them down. Someone tomorrow should howl for my thieving, but I couldn't help that. Trying to get Benedict into leathers was no easy business and he cried to have himself so constricted, he split them a bit, but at least was mostly covered now.

A march of Iremonger police came rushing by, men in brass helmets, all in a worry. We'd go the other way to them, shouldn't like to find them face to face.

'If anyone asks you anything, Benedict,' I said, 'say you've just come in from the sorting and your leathers have been that ripped up. It's not too far now, the boarding house is the far edge of town, close to Bayleaf House.'

We passed into another street. Police whistles were going off in the distance, not for us though, nothing for us to worry over.

'Go home,' Benedict said.

'I'm trying,' I said. 'I am so turned around.'

'Go home,' he said again.

'Hold on a while, Benedict, everything shall come right, I think it shall.'

'No, no. Go home!'

I turned to him then, looked hard at him. He wasn't talking about me or even himself, he was talking to a trail of rubbish that seemed to be following him.

'Go home!' he cried and kicked out at it, and the things seemed to disperse, only to gather up again a small while later, to do it on the sly, when Benedict had turned around.

'Is following me,' he said.

'What is?' I asked.

'It misses me. It calls me back.'

'What is, Benedict?'

'The Heap is, is crying for me.'

'It's just rats, isn't it? They will follow a person if they get a fancy.'

'No, it's rubbish,' he said sadly. 'Likes me, always has.'

'Bits from the heaps you mean?'

'Yes, yes, Heaps bits.'

'Tell them to go away.'

'Am trying! Go home!' he called and for a moment the trail dispersed, only to begin forming itself, and to grow larger this time, just around the corner.

'Let us move faster, Benedict, let us run a little.'

'Is begging me,' he said.

We began to pick up our pace but the trail of rubbish followed after, growing, but always, for now, some little way behind us, but growing in size and, I suppose, in confidence. What a welcome home this is, I thought.

We were back near the Corn Exchange then, the old place where the heaps bits used to be weighed and counted up, long disused that was, even when I was a girl. There was a wheelbarrow in front of it. Someone had just left a wheelbarrow there. As we came a little closer I saw that something was in the wheelbarrow. Some pile of clothing, I thought at first, only then that pile moved, slumped forward a bit, and then I understood it was a person, leaning forward, a person with a balding head who seemed to be in communication with a seagull. Yes, a fat seagull padded around the wheelbarrow, cawing and screeching. At last the man in the wheelbarrow waved his hand and the seagull ran down the street and heaved itself into the air.

The man sat up, looked about him, east and west, what a shiny moon face it was, grinning it was, then I saw the eyes. I'd know him any day. I'd know him by his eyes. He was a cruel one from the House, nearly had me before, on account of the doorknob I took a shine to. Didn't have anything with me much then did I? Oh no, nothing much to speak of, just some pilfered leathers and some man with half the dirt heaps stuck to him and the other half in pursuit. Nothing to declare, no, sir, no, nothing at all.

How he sat up, the blind one in his wheelbarrow.

'Who's there?'

I came no further forwards, pushed Benedict back a bit. But behind him the heaps came on, through the street we'd just quit, tumbling on in after us.

'Who's there? Who's new there?' He put his head out at an angle so the ear could hear the better. 'Such Foulsham calling. Can't hear right, but was there, a moment, did I catch: Iremonger?'

He sat still amongst all the clattering, all that smashing. 'Dunnult?' he cried. 'Where are you, Dunnult?'

There was an officer come running.

'Where've you been?'

'Just patrolling, sir, as you said, giving you some space.'

'There's something wrong here, something very unnatural. Something disturbed and hurt. I never like being out in these streets, would much rather stay indoors. I couldn't catch its name, but there's something very wrong with it, terrible pain and anger. No, no, come, come Dunnult, wheel me on, this town's gone all to hell!'

The wheelbarrow squeaked off into the night, and we could on ourselves. The pursuing dirt had reached our feet by then, was tangling around them, was over us, was lapping there, we only just kicked it off, I reckon, and ran on before it grew any bolder.

Our feet too noisy down the streets. And after it the tumble-crash of objects.

A small blue-glass bottle dislodged itself from the pile and flew at my head.

'Ow!' I cried, picking up the bottle, an old poison one it was, it had marked upon its side NOT TO BE TAKEN. I threw it down again, it rolled away with a greater speed than it should have. 'That hurt!'

'It don't like you,' said Benedict.

'I don't like it,' I said.

'It hates you,' he said.

'Thanks, thanks a lot.'

'Is jealous.'

'What on earth for?'

'It blames you.'

'Blames me for what?'

'For stealing me.'

'I didn't steal you.'

'It thinks you did, maybe you did.'

Round the corner there was noise in the street, such a different sound, the noise of people all bunched up together. How I cheered to hear it! Yes! We might try that, I thought, some company to hide in. I grabbed hold of one of Benedict's arms and quickly pulled him along the way and then ducked quick inside a building, slamming the door behind me, instantly there was a thumping on the door. But it could not break through. We were in a public house. I'd been inside this place when I was a child, sitting with my father: THE HEAP'S REST.

An Iremonger Counterfeit

12

IN WHICH A PROMISE IS MADE AND SOMETHING COMES UNDONE

Continuing the narrative of Clod Iremonger

The Tailor Strikes a Bargain

How he was crumpled upon the floor, the Tailor of Foulsham, his scissors kicked far from his hands.

'Wilfred Pilcher,' I said to the glove that had thrown itself into the Tailor's mouth, 'Wilfred, you may come out now, I thank you. Let the fellow breathe.'

A small and dirty glove fell down, crawled out from under the pillow case and scuttled back into the straw.

'Devil! You very devil!' called the Tailor from underneath Mr Sandford, the old pillow cover.

'I am a friend of things,' I said. 'I do thank you Mr Sandford,

Horace, Elsa, Wilfred, I thank you most awfully!'

'You are that welcome, sir.'

'Glad to be of service.'

'Most gratifying.'

'Please,' called the Tailor, 'call them off, call off your things, get them from me!'

'They've never done that before,' I said. 'I've heard them, I've always heard them, but I've never had them move before, not on my account. The truth is, Mr Erkmann, I'm that astounded. I'm quite impressed!'

'Take them off, call them off!'

'You did provoke me, sir, you must admit to it.'

'You're an Iremonger!'

'I am, sir, it seems even more certain now. In truth, sir, I run from my family. I do not love them very much.'

'Get them off!'

'You must promise, Mr Erkmann, to behave, then they may stand down.'

'I promise,' came his cracked voice.

'Very well then, Mr Sandford, if you wouldn't mind overly.'

'I like to do it,' said Mr Sandford. 'I could quite take his breath from him.'

'Better not, I think, Mr Sandford, on the whole. Do come away now.'

The pillow case blew upwards of a sudden as if by a sharp wind and floated down upon the floor, quiet and still again, a pillow case. The Tailor sat up then, coughed and heaved, his very body rattling. Looking about him much disturbed, 'Indeed,' he said at last, 'you are an Iremonger. I know your family and their business. There are of you ones that can move glass, and them that have a way with metal, or porcelain, and some that can only summon newspaper. I have seen one of your family walk the grounds within the railings of Bayleaf House with ten and more footstools lapping at her feet, and one solemn man who seemed to go a-wandering with a hatstand. You are not a proper people, I think. You oughtn't to be let alone. You should be done away with.'

'We are not all of us, I think,' I said, 'not all so bad. My Cousin Tummis was a very decent fellow, only he was drowned, you see. Ormily, she's a good sort . . .'

'Listen hard, use those precious ears of yours,' said Alexander Erkmann. 'I'll tell you a family story. One to warm your illbred heart.'

'Oh dear, I do not think I shall like it much.'

'Those people that I kill, Clod Iremonger, they are not real people. Your family made them in Bayleaf House. They put them together out of rubbish, they made them from the heaps, to do their bidding. They are among us, these non-people, walking among us, everywhere about us. Slowly, slowly they have been populating Foulsham. They are very like us, indeed they are very clever now, at first they were not, at first they might catch a part of themselves upon a nail, for example, sticking unseen out of a wall and that nail should snag their shirt and then the thing should simply come apart, their insides should pool out of them, sawdust or stones or old cracks of glass, all that they are comes out and spews upon the floor and there is their clothing before us, quite deflated, a person who only a moment ago was sitting beside you. But he has grown better since then, your grandfather. He has found another way. Listen now, Clod Iremonger, harken to this.'

'I do hear, sir, your unhappy history.'

'There are pipes, pipes all over Bayleaf House. Umbitt suffers the children to come unto him, and the children are instructed to breathe into those pipes, that is all, just to breathe, and as they breathe into those pipes, at the other end is a dummy, a thing of human shape but with no life to it, no life at all, but that child he breathes through the pipe, and the child's breath is pumped into the dummy and slowly the dummy inflates, with each breath it has more life, and begins after a time to breathe all of its own, and to take the breath out of the child. One child may have breath enough to make several dummies. Until that child, that child at the other end has had the childhood sucked right out of it.'

'He murders them!'

'No, I cannot say that, it should be a kindness to murder them perhaps. He pulls all the youth out of them, he sucks it out and takes it from them so that after they are left older and deader. Good for working perhaps, but of such small intelligence, they are content to be pushed back and forth. Their eyes are grey and their souls broken, they do not complain. They go on and on until they fall down, and never know why. They often fall to the diseases of Foulsham, they do not last so very long. They tumble into objects within months more often than not. And that is the other terrible prospect about the false people, they spread the disease, their breathing spreads it.'

Very quietly I whispered, 'My family does this?' In the darkness of that hovel, the glove, the plank, the nail, the pillow cover crept into the depths.

'In Bayleaf House, they do it,' said the Tailor. 'And since the children have breathed into the counterfeit people, the counterfeit people are so much the greater, they are almost impossible to spot. Those strange people are much stronger now. They have leather skin many of them, but I knock them down, I unstitch them. Their breath, when they breathe, comes out a slight smoke, like a small fire. It's a little dark smoke their breathing is, but often so small as not to be seen. But I find them, I know them well enough. I was a murderer in my day, from Germany, town of Gelnhausen, I slit a man's throat in an argument grown out of hand, and fleeing to London I stayed awhile, but being traced, I ran to Filching and there I was found by the Iremonger gatherers, and straightway made a letter opener. But, Clod Iremonger, I mean to make amends, and I have done my best, Clod Iremonger, but I am losing this battle. I cannot forever fight that troublesome flask.'

'I shun them, Mr Erkmann, my family. I'll leave here, I'll find Lucy, my friend Lucy, I don't know how. I'll find her and then we'll get out of here somehow and then never see them again, never hear of them, we'll go so far . . .'

'You'll leave them, while they hurt people so?'

'It is terrible. I do see . . .'

'Though they stamp upon lives, and build up a great army of unnatural people, though they spread their foulness all about? They shan't stop, Clod Iremonger, though they are out of your sight. They mean to go on at it, to go on and get strong at it, and then on they'll move into London with all their soulless tribe and on they'll go all over the country, all through Europe, and at last, they'll find you, they'll come to you sudden!'

'My family.'

'Your *family*.'

'I think then, I think they must be stopped. You must do it, sir, you're certainly the fellow.'

'I've not the strength any more.'

'Then whoever shall, if not you?'

'Who indeed, Clod Iremonger?'

'Your look,' I said, feeling a horror mounting inside me, 'your look seems to say . . . that I must.'

'Yes, Clod Iremonger, I think you must. You have your Iremonger talents to you, of that there is no doubt. Put them to better use.'

'Oh,' I said, 'I'm not your general heroic stuff.'

'No, you are not.'

'I'm not one to wield the scissors.'

'No, you are not.'

'Not fierce, you see.'

'I do see that.'

'Not particular brave.'

'No, not particular.'

'It is terrible what they do . . .'

'It is.'

'If it is the absolute truth.'

'It is, and you know it.'

'I suspect it.'

'You do.'

'I do, I do.'

'Well then.'

'Well then, well then . . .'

'Well then?'

'Well then, I suppose I must.'

'Then we're of a mind, you and I.'

I looked up at the taut man and thought what strange bedfellows war gives a person. I shook his hand then, long and thin and cold and absolutely upsetting to the touch.

Well, Clod, here's a murderer beside you. What a daguerreotype that should be, and what's at the end of this long trail for you, I wonder, the hangman's rope?

Boots in the mud broke up our shaking, men marching by and a young voice calling out.

The Tailor had one long finger to his lips.

'You cloth soldiers,' called an officer beyond our hovel. 'March now, hurry, vermin. How I hate you! That I should have to have you for my companions. Look smart, will you? We're after a gloomy boy, you maggots, dark hair, we've got his plug back at the factory, so he'll be turning soon enough if he hasn't already. That and the Tailor, do you hear, he's here somewhereabouts. Come on, leatherbags, you find him or you'll answer to me. Spread out, I want every bit of this turd-town searched.'

My cousin Moorcus, I should know him anywhere.

'I've a new gun here,' Moorcus continued. 'I'm very fond of this here pistol. It's so new and I've such an itch to use it. I'll call it my new birth object.'

'But, sir.'

'Shut up, Toastrack, or I'll brain you! Listen, sackmen, I'm that fond of this pistol. Here, what a thing it is. It's a

Beaumont-Adams it is, smuggled in from London. Give me a chance. Give me a reason to be upset with you, any one of you, and this shall make a nice hole in your face!'

A brief silence after that.

'You there, what's your name?' Moorcus called.

'Giles Clompton, sir.'

'Got your whistle about you?'

'Sir.'

'Search the huts along here, any trouble blow you, call out, man. Go, maggot, slug, earthworm, go on! The rest of you, follow me I say! Come along, Toastrack! Keep close will you?'

Boots going off, and then one man marching about, swinging the neighbouring doors open, looking inside.

'It'll be my turn to show you something in just a minute, Clod Iremonger,' the Tailor whispered. 'Quiet, quiet.'

The door of our hut swung open, an Iremonger officer was there with a lantern, shining it about. I heard no sound coming from him, no noise at all. He stepped in, kicked some of the straw on the ground. And the Tailor ventured forward.

It didn't take long.

It was all over in a horrible moment.

A sudden flashing of something bright and metallic. The scissors snapped hard on the officer, they made a quick puncture through the coat. And the officer, he just stood there, looking so confused, not hurt, only very confused, and a terrible smell came off him, like that of rubbish trapped inside a metal bin for ages and suddenly lifting the lid, the stale air escaping out into the night. From that hole began to pour out bits of old ash and burnt-up wood, much rotten paper and material, some chips of old crockery, all tumbling out on the floor.

'Whatever have you done?' said the officer, his voice perturbed. 'I seem to be, how now, I seem to be emptying . . .'

The Tailor stepped up and with one swift and thorough gesture took hold of the cut and made a huge rip of it, now all tumbled out and the officer grew less and less.

'Oh,' he said, 'oh, I seem to be coming undone!'

The black gas was coming off the fellow, the bad stink. He looked up at the man who had ripped him.

'You're, you're . . .' but his voice was getting weaker, 'you're . . .'

'Your tailor,' said the Tailor.

But as the officer collapsed upon the floor, a wisp of black gas from his nose, like a slug, and it crawled its way rapidly along his collapsed chest, and it found its way into the whistle that hung on a chain around his neck and that gas, it somehow blew upon the whistle, it blew hard, and with that final awful excursion the whole body of the thing slumped down lifeless.

'Come, Clod, they shall be upon us in a moment!'

The Heap's Rest –

A Foulsham Public House

13

BEER AND BED

Continuing the narrative of Lucy Pennant

Sawdust thick on the floor, hunched people propped over tin mugs, some red in the face, some yellow, women sweating by their men, a lone child being given sips to keep him quiet. The publican, the same publican I had seen when I lived with my parents, a familiar face amongst all those faces, there he was! A bit older perhaps, a bit larger maybe, a bit more bowed but the same man, and his wife, where was she? I remember her too; a thinner woman, her hair was falling out even then – her face resembled a chamber pot. We used to laugh about it, me and my school friends, I shouldn't now. I couldn't see her anywhere. But on the bar rested a large enamel pot.

It was noisy inside in that dim place, else our entrance should perhaps have caused more upset. There was a man singing out one of the heap ballads and all were listening or singing with him.

Deep in the dirtland, I was a-shifting,
When in the darkness, I found a-trickling,
A beautiful maiden, all dressed in white linen,
She smiles at me lovely and calls me to come in.
I'll never go picking, no more, no more.
I'll never go picking no more.

Such people, my people, all huddled together, banging on the table, clinking tankards,

She walks further out in the darkness and deep.
She walks on such light skipping feet.
And I follow her stumbling,
While the weather is rumbling.
I'll never go picking no more, no more.
I'll never go picking no more.

Some people had hung their old hats and coats up by the door, the raining heap weather collected in puddles beneath them, soot, bits of old papers (love letters, newspapers) got up in the heap winds, shards of glass, old rusted nails, bones, scraps of cloth. It was like home. How it warmed me to see such things.

I took an old cap off a peg. I slapped the hat on Benedict's head to disguise him a bit, to at least cover up the beetles that still crawled about his face.

I follow on after each clumsy step,
And further and further out of my depth.
She calls me, she calls me, my darling my dear,

And on do I follow though the heaplands I fear.
I'll never go picking, no more, no more.
I'll never go picking no more.

I went in among them and pulled Benedict after, shuffling by, smiling at them and saying 'How do' like I'd never been away. All the while the song went on and for the moment the knocking on the door was not heard above it. I tugged Benedict on, he was shivering under the coat, quite in a terror.

There was a way out the back, I'd used it as a child. I was making my way towards it when the publican called out, 'Now then, what's your measure?'

'Two jars,' said I, turning back.

He filled the drinks. I looked hard into his face. Recognise me, I thought. Please, please recognise me. But his bloodshot eyes barely seemed to notice anything.

'Thruppence,' he said.

'Thruppence,' I repeated to Benedict. 'You must pay the man.'

For hours we walked on, through bog and through creek,
When finally she stopped, we were out there so deep.
She turned around then, and I saw her so close,
She was all a skeleton, a dead person, a ghost.
I'll never go picking, no more, no more.
I'll never go picking no more.

What a shambles that caused from poor Benedict. His claws dug into the pockets beneath his leathers, pulled out bits of china, a few shining buttons, some earth, a portion of a seagull, a charred puppet's head.

She grabbed at me fast, I felt her embrace,
And I screamed as I stared at her own bony face.
She took all my breathing, she took all my breath,
And alone then she left me, alone with my death.
I'll never go picking, no more, no more,
I'll never go picking no more.

Then came out Benedict's money, a torrent of it, clanging upon the table, and then all stopped and then all did watch.

'Only thruppence,' I said, passing the coins over. 'The rest may go back in the pocket.' I shoved the coins away. 'He's newly arrived,' I tried to explain, 'from Russia originally. Very new to Filching, very new indeed.'

'Filching?' said the publican. 'We don't say that no more. It's Foulsham called, where've you been?'

'Do you know me? I was here with my father.'

'Could be,' he said. 'Could be yes, could be no. Wait up, wait up a minute, was that a half sovereign I saw in that pile? There's to be no half sovereigns in this house!'

At the mention of the coin they all set to murmuring, eyes flashing in the shadows, and then a young spotty man with an umbrella got up from a table and moved hurriedly towards the door.

Someone called to us, 'Hey, wait a minute, that's my hat that is. He's stole my hat!'

Just then the umbrella man reached the door and took the handle and pulled it open and then what a mound poured in over him.

There were screams of, 'A Gathering! A Gathering!'

'Quick! This way!' I cried, grabbing hold of Benedict and pulling him to the other door, away, away from the heap that was pouring in. Through a side door we ran, certain to shut it firm behind us, and we were in the street, and there at the far end, up the steep hill, was the boarding house. Home! There was the lettering, much patched up, much added to, upon the building,

MRS WHITING'S CLEAN HOUSE
ROOMS TO LET
MOST REASONABLE RATES
APPLY WITHIN
PORTER ON DUTY AT ALL TIMES
CLEAN!
NO DISEASE
ONLY THE HEALTHY NEED APPLY

'Come now, Benedict, before those things find us. Onwards!'

The side door opened behind us.

'Come on! Come on!' I cried.

A man stumbled out. 'My hat!' he called. 'You got my hat!'

'Let him have it,' I said. 'Give him the sodding hat.

'Our mistake,' I said. 'It's so like his. Beg pardon.'

I gave it over.

'Who's that with you?' he asked. 'Who's your fella? I think I know him . . . there's something familiar . . .'

'Mind your own,' I said. 'Good night.'

'Wait up,' the man said, jogging alongside us. 'There's something wrong with him and all. What's happened to you, mate? What happened?'

'He's ill, isn't he. He's turning you fool,' I said. 'I shouldn't come close.'

Well, that stopped the chap, he even handed the hat back to me – 'Maybe's not my hat after all. You're welcome to it so ever it were mine.' – and went rushing the other way.

'Here we are then,' I said. 'Tug that hat down.'

I pulled on the bell. Nothing. The wind was picking up all around us, blowing objects about the street, clanging, and clattering against the buildings, just a little way away there came a large crashing of glass. I pulled on the bell. Sheets of newspapers were dancing in the wind, pages were somersaulting down the street, but more and more of them, as if it were snowing. I pulled on the bell again.

'They're coming, they're coming!' cried Benedict.

'Come on, answer! Why won't you answer?'

There was a shadow amassing around the corner, something was coming, something very large.

'Come on, oh come on!' I cried, pulling on the door.

The shadow was coming closer, a whole great clot of things gathering up and rushing forwards I pulled on the bell.

And then at last there was someone the other side, an old voice, 'Who's there that's not weather? What do you want?'

'Is that Mrs Whiting? Is it?'

'Who's asking? I've a great gun in my hands, my husband's blunderbuss. Be off with you!'

'It's Lucy Pennant.'

166

'Lucy Pennant? No, no, she's dead. Dead and buried and out the game!'

'No, Mrs Whiting, at least not quite yet. Will you open the door please?'

'I'm full up.'

'We have money, Mrs Whiting, lots of money.'

The door opened and we tumbled in. The old lady shut it behind her, and I helped her to push the bolts true.

'Lucy Pennant! It *is* Lucy Pennant! Only you're . . . well, well . . . you stink. You'll smell my house down.'

There she was. She seemed barely to have aged. The old woman in her finery, quite the best dressed woman in the whole town. Quite the shock to see her, to be recognised again.

'Been travelling, Mrs Whiting, but home now. Need a room.'

'Need a bath,' she said.

There was knocking on the door, light this time, like pebbles. Oh, it's cunning, that heap, I thought. It knows a thing.

'Don't answer,' I said. 'Please don't.'

I took some money from Benedict. I counted a deal out, almost half a quid.

'So much currency!' the old woman muttered.

'There's more,' I said, 'much more.'

'Well, Lucy, well, pet, let's situate you, shall we?' she said, shuffling on.

'Thank you, thank you kindly.'

'I'll give you old Mr Heighton's rooms. They need an airing but you'll not grumble over that.'

'Dear Mr Heighton, what happened to him?'

'He turned to a brass fender last spring. Saw it coming.'

'Poor Mr Heighton.'

'Who's to say? Better out of it, I think. There's a new porter, pet, name of Rawling. No doubt you'll see him in the morning. He went out drinking before the sun gave up and no doubt he can't find his way home. He always does in the end though, comes back to me of a morning, bad tempered and sorrowful, and swears he'll never be at it again, but he is of course after a week or two. Lucy, I am sorry about your parents, such a shock. Such good workers, such clean people too.'

'Thank you, Mrs Whiting, that's very kind of you.'

'I said to my Mr Whiting, I said,' she said, 'never were ones for portering as those Pennants, never were such as them.'

'That's kind.'

'Good people.'

'Thank you.'

'Who's he then, under the cap? Don't say much, do he?'

'This is Mr . . . Mr Tipp,' I said. 'He's very shy.'

She turned the corner. 'Well then, here we are.'

'You're very kind, Mrs Whiting. I'm glad to be back.'

'Welcome home, Lucy Pennant. Welcome home, Mr Tipp. Perhaps we shall have some order in this place now you're back inside it.'

I closed the door. All Mr Heighton's things were still in the room and all very dusty. We both had the same worry, and both looked a little through the faded curtains. A gathering had amassed outside, that thing of things was swirling on the street beneath us. For a moment it seemed to me to take the shape and look of Benedict, as if in its misery it were imitating him, showing him beating his fists in agony against his head and then no sooner had it assumed its vague human shape than, with a sorrowful groan, it spat apart as if detonating, making a terrible crashing sound all along the street.

'Go to sleep!' cried Mrs Whiting out into the night. 'It isn't decent!'

Rippit Iremonger, found at last

14

BEFORE THE SUN RISES

Continuing the narrative of Clod Iremonger

The Last Post

'Come, Clod Iremonger, come,' the Tailor called. 'They shall be upon us in a moment!'

I went with the Tailor then, back out through the lane, people running, officers there.

Lights behind and more whistles blowing and calls of, 'Stop! Murderer! Stop! Stop or I shoot!'

Behind us guns now, guns at us exploding. Chips and dust coming off the wall from where the bullets hit. They'll murder us this night, they shall do it.

He knew his way, the great length of Tailor, and how I must rush to keep up with his long strides.

'Hurry! Hurry! If we can but reach the house, come, Clod!'

But as we ran along through obscure ways, stepping over

sleeping bodies, even into grim buildings with families huddled by a small fire, or holding in their filthy arms some object that had once been a loved one of theirs, I became more and more certain that it was not I that needed to hurry up, but the Tailor who was beginning to slow.

Ever since we were on the chase my cousin's voice had grown stronger and louder and was calling out now, as if to give us away, 'Rippit Iremonger! Rippit Iremonger! Rippit Iremonger!'

And beneath the tall man, rattling through his ribs as he panted on, came, as if in unhappy answer, 'Letter opener, Letter opener, Letter opener.'

Those two voices in terrible conversation with each other.

We were in a tenement house of some kind then, smashing by people who one and all screamed to see the Tailor. But always behind us the wails of Foulsham beggars and the calling of Moorcus and his officers on the hunt. There was a great tall cupboard before us that I heard moaning its name: 'Sergeant Clark.'

I stopped before it.

'Please Sergeant, if you could, I should be ever most obliged if you could lay yourself flat and so block the way.'

'Sir, do you bid me?'

'I do, Sergeant, if you shall.'

'Sir, I shall,' came the instant response and when we had just cleared him he came crashing down the way, and now none might follow us on this route.

We came out of the tenement through a back door and then a wide street. How naked we were, running across such a street and the day coming on, the sun beginning to strain through the dirty air of Foulsham, sending its yellow light down upon us like a massive torch pointing us out, saying here they are, get them, look how they progress up the hill!

'Rippit Iremonger! Rippit Iremonger!'

'Letter opener! Letter opener!'

'Rippit Iremonger! RIPPIT IREMONGER!'

'Rippit, Rippit!' I cried. 'Be quiet, I command you to be quiet.'

But in response there was a louder wailing, 'RIPPITIREMONGER!'

Police whistles behind us calling out, police on their tramp, 'Which way? Which way?' they called and the people answered them with awful speed, 'There they go! There! There!'

Our shadows, our shadows such long shadows up the hill, up the wide street, climbing the high ground towards the factory. Alexander's shadow so long and thin stretching almost the length of the hill as if it had arrived at the place already, so far before us, but that shadow was suddenly wavering now, growing weaker. Was it the sun on that shadow or was it Rippit biting at it?

'See, Clod Iremonger, see far up there near the top, a tall white house at the back of the square? Do you see it?'

'Yes, sir. Yes I do.'

'There I live, there I hide, in the attic at the top.'

'Come on, sir,' I cried. 'Do but come on, they are fast behind!'

'I weary, I do weary now.'

'RIPPITIREMONGER! RIPPITIREMONGER!'

'Letter opener! Letter opener!'

'Clod Iremonger, Clod fellow, run now. There is a hatch, it

looks like a coal chute leading down the building, but it is not, it is a thin passageway between walls where you can climb up and come out unseen in the attic, my place, my hiding place these five years.'

'I understand, sir, but please come on!'

'I am out of breath!'

'RIPPITIREMONGER! RIPPITIREMONGER!'

From below in the town, the sun coming up, a great calling out, and then a terrible echoing of that inner noise, the same words spoken out, out in the open. Someone calling out to us in response,

'Rippit! Rippit Iremonger! I hear Rippit calling!'

'It's Uncle Idwid!' I cried. 'He has heard Rippit!'

'I am going, Clod, I am going now.'

'No, sir, please, please do not leave me.'

'Run now, run fast, find the place.'

'Please sir!'

'RIPPITIREMONGERRIPPITIREMONGER!'

'You must stop them, Clod.'

'Rippit Iremonger, I heard you now!' came Idwid from down the way. 'I am coming! I come to you!'

'LETTEROPENER! LETTEROPENER!'

'RIPPITIREMONGERRIPPITIREONGER!'

'Run, Clod, for all your life. I am going back down the hill.'

He turned then, the Tailor of Foulsham, and began his descent, his scissors out, raised before him. I ran on, I ran higher, tears down my face.

Such noises, such calling out behind me, all the police running from the small streets all gathering up at him, snapping at his heels, and people at their windows screaming, all around him. All calling, all calling, all calling,

'The Tailor! The Tailor! The Tailor! There he is! Get him! Bring him down!'

One last look back. I saw the Tailor, tall amongst them all. His head went back, there was a terrible snapping sound, more snaps and cracks going off as if someone were breaking sticks, one after the other snapping his bones, and with each snap the lean man twisted and lurched and fell down so that he was ever smaller, ever less himself, the snapping creating a blur of tearing clothes and flesh, moving so fast that I could no longer see him, he was only fast, toppling weather, and when the weather had stopped, he was no longer there. He had clattered to the ground.

And then, in all that shrieking and clamouring, one piercing cry of 'Alexander Erkmann!'

He had tumbled out of himself, he was a knife again. And out of that cry came a voice from a relative of mine, a small, wide man, strangely small and strangely wide, not a person you had ever seen the like of before, saying over,

'Rippit Iremonger. Rippit Iremonger.'

'Nephew!' called Idwid. 'My nephew! Back again!'

I was at the top of the hill, along the square. The white house.

MRS WHITING'S CLEAN HOUSE
ROOMS TO LET

So much filth and dirt all about it, I picked my way through. They'd be up, the Iremonger police in their hunt, up in a moment after me. I found it at last, the coal hatch. I was in then, inside, so black, so dark. I crawled through, there was a ladder just as he said, up I went, up and up, feeling the walls should give way and squash me any moment. But then the ladder stopped, I found the tunnelling and fell out into a fireplace, into an attic room.

Part Two

The Boarding House

Binadit

15

HOME AGAIN, HOME AGAIN

Continuing the narrative of Lucy Pennant

It didn't feel any more certain in the morning. I hadn't supposed it would really. The day, when it came, was grey and windy. The house shook with the wind, the windows rattled. It rained and it rained. Only after a bit did I realise it wasn't water that was knocking against the windows, not raindrops, it was heapbits. Old scraps of clothing, glass, nails, shattered bits clinked against the windows. All felt miserable and unwelcome. And familiar too, sounds from my childhood.

I was home. Home at last and after such a journey. I lay on Mr Heighton's bed and looked up at the ceiling, trying to find some meaning, some pattern in the cracks there. I hadn't known idleness like this for so long. I thought that perhaps if I was really still, if I kept absolutely still then maybe none of it would ever have happened.

Then maybe Mother and Father would come up the stairs

and scold me for being in Mr Heighton's room, then maybe Mr Heighton would come back too and no longer be a brass fender, then I should never have gone to the orphanage and Cusper Iremonger should never have picked me for a servant instead of Mary Staggs, that spiteful auburn creature, then I should never have gone serving out in that twisted mansion, then I should never have met Florence Balcombe, who was my friend, and likely she should have been better off without me, that there had never been a moustache cup, that there had never been a storm, such a terrible storm, that never poor Tummis should have drowned out there, sucked down into the deeps and smashed by them, that none of it had ever happened, that I had remained only and forever here, with my mother and my father and all was safe and ever as it had been and none of it, none of it, had ever happened.

I wondered if that could ever be, if it might all be cancelled out, if only I kept very still. Perhaps if I lay still, then it might all go away again. Only if it did, if none of it was ever true, if objects weren't people, if all was safe and true and trustful, then, oh then, oh, then, I should never, never have met him.

'Clod!' I cried, as if he was actually somewhere near, and then I fell out of bed.

It had all happened. Every horror moment of it, 'course it had. I'd never have been with him otherwise. No going back, no scrabbling backwards for safety, only forwards from this black spot, from this bad space – there had been worse, I knew that, darker wheres than this one. I made this promise. Clod. Clod, we've tumbled into this together, and must venture to untangle ourselves from it.

I must find him; I promised I would. My leg hurt, ached like it was dying. Painful to stand on it. So what, I thought, may that hurting be a reminder to you, keep you going, got to keep on going.

'Ow!' came a wild voice, quite shocking me.

Oh. Yes. Certainly all true then. Every last bit of it was true, because there upon the floor was a mound of rubble rubbish, and that unhappy collection was alive, was breathing. Indeed I had just stepped upon it.

'Ow!'

'Mr Tipp, I presume,' I said to him. 'Morning to you.'

'Where?'

'Home,' I said. 'We've come home.'

I looked out of the window onto the street, the people shuffling about in the early day one man, an official type, at the corner, looking up at the house as if he was watching it. I looked across up the hill, through the gates of Bayleaf House, at the great building there spewing black smoke, thick with its own weather. I looked down. There was stuff around the boarding house, more around it than any other building, twice as much maybe, like they were coming gradually, those heap bits, sneaking their way there. I looked back at Benedict. I'd need to disguise him better. Couldn't do anything with him like that. I'd give him the best disguise possible: I'd clean him.

'I mean to civilise you, Benedict.'

'Not to do it.'

'Oh yes, I mean to clip you and snip you and scrub you clean.'

'Shall hurt?'

'Yes, I believe it shall.'

'I'll eat you.'

'We'll see about that.'

'I'm hongry.'

'This is 1876, my man. Time to get modern.'

A fat beetle perambulating upon Benedict's person came to his attention, and he pinched the thing in his claws and proceeded to eat it. Not an auspicious beginning.

'I shall need help,' I said.

I bade Benedict keep himself quiet in the back room and positioned myself at Mr Heighton's door. I was waiting to see who I might spy upon the stairs, who else lived there, who was new and who was remembered. This was my turf. I knew it, every part of it, every corner, every flea almost, you could say.

Sat there at the keyhole upon a stool, I saw old Mrs Walker with her pet rat Solomon passing by. God, how that thing had grown bald and shabby since I last saw it. Snappy little thing that rat was, been at my heels, hadn't it. I could almost remember the feel of its teeth even now.

She used to pay me in sugar cubes to take the thing out and walk it around the block. She did love it so, poor thing limping along. There's many of the lonely people of Filching seek a pet for company, the cats of Filching are too dangerous to befriend, and the last Filching dog died its death before I was born, all of them eaten by the cats or the rats, or the people too, but the rats could be tamed up to a point, they were all right.

Off she went, Mrs Walker and her rat, wheezing up the stairway, both of them sounding like they had the same wrecked lungs. Well they couldn't help it, I'd leave them be. Good to see you, someone else from before. 'Good morning,' I whispered, so quiet that I should never be heard.

Not long after I saw Mr and Mrs Harding on the stairs, all buckled up in their leathers they were, off to the morning shift, both of them coughing and looking grim. Never liked them much, they ticketed both their children. And thereafter everyone in the block blanked them. Others in leathers followed, all off sorting. Didn't know them, new people, at least the ones with faces on show. Many were already hidden beneath buckled leather masks to keep them from getting cut. All must sort unless they had a pass. Children too most days, when there wasn't school.

Wouldn't do to stop anyone if they were off sorting. Get reported for holding someone up, there was a heavy fine for that. No, no, leave them be. Soon enough the house would be emptied and only the old and the young would be left inside, the old women and men telling the young unlikely stories of old Filching, of bygone ogres and the like, of the Iremonger family and what they did to things in their dark properties.

After a bit there were more lively feet on the stairs, and a girl about my own age came into view, tugging her younger brother behind her. It was Jenny Ryall and her little brother Dick, who everyone always called Bug because he used to catch roaches and race them. Earned quite a bit doing that, used to collect bets from all of the boarding house, till it was stopped by a policing Iremonger after the new rule about no gatherings of people being allowed, no more than three persons together at a time. Still he was called Bug, even after, it had stuck.

'Oy!' I whispered through the keyhole. 'Oy! Jen! Over here.'

That stopped her, what a frown on her dear old face, and Bug's too.

'Who's there?' she asked.

'Who do you think?' I asked.

'Wait a minute,' she said. 'It can't be.'

'What is it, Jen?' said Bug. 'You said we'd be late.'

'There's someone behind the door there,' said Jen.

'Is it Heighton's ghost?' asked Bug.

'But it can't be,' said Jen.

'Yes,' I said, 'it bloody is.'

'Who bloody is it?' asked Bug.

'It's only bloody Lucy Pennant!' said Jen.

'Bloody Moory! I thought she'd been dead by now,' said Bug.

'Well, I'm not,' I said. 'Not yet any rate. Come in. Quickly!'

In they rushed and the door closed after.

'God, do you stink,' said Bug.

'Thanks,' I said. 'Nice to see you and all.'

'What happened to you, Lucy?' asked Jenny. 'Your hair's wilder than ever it used to be.'

'That,' I said, 'is the very least of it.'

'What happened to you? How did you get like that?'

'Is quite a tale I admit.'

'You haven't run away, have you? They'll come for you if you have. What are you wearing, that's a maid's dress isn't it? What are you doing in that? Come along, spill it.'

And I told her, well, some of it, but then Bug called out,

'OH MY BLESSED HEAP! What ever is that?'

Bug, snooping about, had found Benedict.

'Who's there?' screamed Jenny. 'Oh Bug! Come away, run!'

'No, no,' I cried, 'it's all right, please.'

'A Gathering! A Gathering!' screamed Bug.

And then, frightened by the sudden people and their noise, Benedict started screaming too, and all three were at it, until I, screaming over the top of them to shut it quick, managed at last a little peace, but anyone in the house could have heard that, or anyone outside watching it.

'He's with me. He's all right, I promise. He won't hurt you. They won't hurt you, Benedict. Calm please, and quiet.'

'Wherever did you find that?' whispered Bug.

'*Him*,' I said. 'He's called Benedict.'

'You call *that* Benedict? Odd name for it,' said Bug.

'I found him,' I said, 'or at least he found me, out in the heaps. I need to tidy him up. He might startle people as he is.'

'Well, I never,' said Bug. 'I'm Bug, by the by, how do?'

He put his hand out for Benedict to shake and Benedict, opening his mouth, nearly bit it off.

'No, Benedict, no!'

'He nearly eat me, he was that bloody close!'

'Now, Bug, don't go on so,' I said. 'There are things he's not used to. He's to be schooled, he's been neglected, but he's all right. Though I do need to clean him up. That's the first thing, and I need soap and a tub, and brushes, and scissors, I think, clippers. Can you help?'

Jenny said she would, Bug thought he might.

'Hang on,' said Jenny. 'Have you papers? Has he?'

'Well,' I said, 'no, not as such.'

'You need papers to be in Foulsham, Lucy. Oh, where've you

been? You can't go anywhere without papers. They're always asking for papers, anyone in the street, not just Iremongers either. Any neighbour may come to any neighbour's house any time of day or night and ask for papers, it's seen as a person's duty. And Rawling, the porter, he's a particular one for doing it, sits at his desk by the door and he sees people's papers as they come in or out. What ever are you going to do?'

And I admit I felt a bit defeated then, and sat down to wonder a little. What was I after all, just Lucy Pennant, nothing more, Lucy Pennant with a strange giant for company. Both of us illegal, both of us apt to be picked up in a moment.

'Well,' I said, after a moment, just to keep going, just so something could be spoken, 'well, what's new, Jenny? What's new in the house? Anything much? I see Mrs Walker's rat's gone bald.'

And Jenny, she sits beside me, and she tells me about those that had turned, about Rawling and his prowling. When I asked after my old friends Anne Dawson and Bess Whitler and even Tom Jackson and the cross-eyed Arthur Beckett, she told me that they had all been ticketed. That their parents had sold them off, every last one of them.

'How ever could they? It's disgusting!' I said.

'Wait a moment, Lucy, not so fast, don't you go judging no one. Not until you know. They put the price of tickets up. It's a lot of money you get for a ticket now, a whole lot, and for some families it's the only choice they have. And besides, when you're ticketed they say you're looked after, you're well fed and educated. And so it's not so easy to argue with, not really. I may get ticketed. I may yet, Bug too, and sometimes I think

I don't mind the idea of it. No, I'll tell you, sometimes I love the idea of it, for then I'll be somewhere other than here. The days will be different, I'll no longer have to go sorting, I'll do things, I'll have a uniform maybe, I'll count, I'll have *meaning*. It will be something at least, something other than day after day in this dreary boarding house, with precious little money and with no space. No, I think, after all, maybe it's not so bad. I'd find Bess. I'd see Anne again.'

'What a business,' I said, and very quietly, because she'd quite broken my heart with her little speech. The house and all of Foulsham were quite going rotten. Poor Jenny was nearly lost to it all. I'd have to bring her back, reel her in, poor doll.

'What about the man at the top?' I said. 'The one who never came out. Is he still there? Remember how we used to creep up and listen out for him, and look through his keyhole, remember that?'

'Mam said it was just the house creaking,' cackled Jenny. 'That no one lived there. That we were just being silly. But no one goes up there, not any more. I shouldn't, not likely. Mrs Walker's rat hisses on the stairs but won't go up. Porter Rawling won't clean there, so it's got worse and worse.'

'Look at the fellow,' Bug said, pointing at Benedict with admiration. 'He's got creepy-crawlies all over him.'

'Yes,' I said, 'they do tend to nest in him. About that soap . . .'

Jenny and Bug went upstairs to their place and fetched some washing things, they said they'd have to take them back when they returned from school in case their parents should notice them gone.

'I'm glad you're back, Lucy,' Jenny said before leaving. 'I'd keep yourself quiet if I were you. Rawling's always snooping and he has the key to this room, has keys to all of them, goes in and out of anywhere without bothering to knock. He's got so rude of late. The tenants complain to Mrs Whiting all the time, but it don't do no good. He's an Iremonger man through and through. I think he may have been behind some of the ticketing if I'm honest. Were hardly any tickets in this house before he came, only the Hardings and they're awful Iremonger in their doings too.'

'Jenny, have you seen any of the children after they went into Bayleaf House, after they were ticketed?'

'No, of course not, they never come out. They've no need to.'

'And do you think, Jenny, that it's a good life stuck inside those walls?'

'Couldn't say, could I? Reckon it is.'

'But what if it isn't?'

'It must be, Lucy, it has to be. There's got to be something for us other than the heaps. There has to be and it's there, through them gates.'

'But what if it isn't?'

'They say it is!'

'But you've never seen anyone after, so how could you know?'

'But then there'd be nothing for us, would there, nothing at all! We can't go out into London. The London wall is guarded and they shoot anyone if he so much as peeps over it. The dirt carts are searched thorough, and all there is, is the heaps for us. So if it isn't better being ticketed, then . . .' Her voice was so quiet now. 'Then there's nothing, is there . . . then it's all hopeless.'

'I know a boy out there in Heap House,' I said, 'one of their own. He believed in them at first, but he found things out, terrible things, and they tried to hunt him down, to shut him up.'

'You met an Iremonger?'

'Yes, I did.'

'I don't believe it.'

'It's true, and we got lost from each other, and I need to find him again.'

'You need to find an Iremonger?'

'He's in trouble, I think, terrible trouble. They'll crush him if they can, though he's of their blood. Maybe they have already. 'Cause he knows things and he can help us. Listen, Jenny, will you do something for me?'

'Depends, doesn't it?'

'Do you think you could get everyone together from school, could we meet somewhere and talk?'

'It's not allowed. There'd be trouble, sure to be.'

'Everyone's so frightened,' I said. 'If we could just somehow get everyone together and talk, we could make things seem clearer, if only we could do that, then maybe we'd start to fight them, to get our people back, to ask, Jenny, at least to ask to see all those children who've been ticketed. Only let us see them, let them come to the gates, then we'd know.'

'They wouldn't like that.'

'No, no they bloody wouldn't, but if no one ever stands up then we'll slowly, one by one, be trampled under, miserable and quiet and broken forever!'

'Well . . .'

191

'Just to talk, Jenny. Let me talk . . .'

'All right, I'll see,' she said, then, 'I'm frightened, to be honest, Lucy. I'm that frightened.'

'Good. I'm glad you are because then you're realising that they like to scare, don't they? And why would they scare if they hadn't something terrible to hide?'

'All right, Luce,' she whispered. 'I'll do me best.'

Bug and Jenny went off to the schoolhouse. Well, I thought, it's a start. It's got to start somewhere. I was even quite proud of myself. We'll form an army, I shouldn't wonder. What a thought! I turned to Benedict sitting on the floor.

'Well then,' I said. 'Are you ready?'

'Wot?'

'Off with them . . . things.'

'They're mine, they live here.'

'They're evicted.'

No sign of that porter yet, so I risked treading out with a couple of buckets, out to the old well in the square. I had them purloined leathers over my old rags, so I looked the part: by which I mean I looked ordinary enough. I left Benedict in the rooms, told him to keep there and still and all, and not look out the window. So.

I pushed the front door open, wouldn't come at first, that much stuff loaded around it, but I heaved the door to, and the stuff fell away. I kicked it and swung the buckets at it. It moved like it was only rubbish blown there, like I was making it all up in my head, only then why was all the rubbish at the boarding house door and none nowhere else? I shoved the door shut behind me, and ploughed over to the well.

I saw the watching man close up. He wasn't looking at me, only at the houses around. He wasn't alone, I noticed then, there were several of them, one at each corner, all looking up, one puffing on a pipe, one eating a Forlichingham bun, the dark treacle of it down his front, but you could tell they weren't proper people, not our lot at all, you could tell by the sheen of them. There was something put on about them, something not of our Foulsham at all, something very Iremonger, I should say. I wondered then if our old boarding house wasn't a deathtrap.

I marched along to the well looking so innocent, my steam coming out of my mouth in the cold morning air, and then I noticed their breath seemed to be coming out black, not white like mine, very queer that. Wasn't natural, was it? What had happened here, since I'd been away?

I got the buckets home, heaved them back. Sure enough, all those things, all them heap bits had got back in front of the door while I wasn't looking, covering over the steps, though I'd kicked them off not two minutes ago. I shoved them along again, though I hated even my old clogs to touch them. I shoved them along, Lord knows I'd scrub myself after touching that. I slammed the door behind me and was up the stairs, and there in Heighton's rooms was Benedict, shaking.

'Gone so long!'

'I'm back now, don't fuss!'

'Worried!'

'I can look after myself.'

I made a good fire and heated the water. I washed myself

first for I certainly I had a need to, and so that seeing me wash, Benedict should know it was all right. I tugged my dress off, what was left of it, and threw it in the fire. I pulled my drawers off, threw them in too. Well then, there I was, naked as the day I was born.

Benedict was staring at me.

'Hongry,' he said. He picked a spider from his hair and nonchalantly chewed on it. 'White and red, aren't you. Not much to you. Not much meat.'

'Will you stop your staring?'

'Like to.'

Well, I got on and washed then, wasn't going to spend any energy on being modest, gone well past that sort of sentiment. I needed to scrub him good and that meant getting him stripped so it seemed stupid to fuss over myself like some modest princess. We're all of us only animals anyway, no good pretending we're not. There's a body under every suit and dress wandering the streets, no matter that they pretend there isn't.

Even Victoria herself has a body under all that black bombazine; even queens got bodies, got blood and skin and all of it. Good to be naked, after the prisoning of clothing, after all. I'm not ashamed of me, not one little bit.

I pulled on one of Jenny's dresses she had brought for me and felt much better, human even. I heated the other bucket, poured it in and then I turned to him.

'Mr Tipp,' I said, 'now then, what are you under all that? Take it off, take it all off.'

But Mr Tipp didn't like to, not one bit. The problem was working out what was him and what was . . . not. The water was black very quickly, and the longer he soaked the more things floated around him. Some bits of things sticking to him came off quite quickly, unglued by the water, but much of it was stuck firm and no amount of scrubbing seemed to help. I do not know how many insects I drowned that day, but there were many and as Benedict lay there splashing about, so splashed the creatures too, some managing to find their way to the bath's edge and, clambering up, won their freedom.

It couldn't be done in one go, he needed a fireman's cannon I think, he needed a surgeon's knife. I couldn't bring him back human, not all at once. I should have to reclaim him very slowly. Bit by bit. Taking it all off in one go might kill the poor thing, be like flaying him. He'd grown into all that, stuff stuck to him and him into stuff, so that they were of a piece. Coaxing the person back had to be done carefully. I knew it wasn't just about the outside of him either, I knew there was the inside too, and that was hurt and strange.

The best cause was to get at his face and hands, the parts of him that would be on display. I took up the scissors. What first I had assumed was his hair at the top of him was actually bits of old wicker mat, I also found about him an embroidered cushion, a lady's hat (remains of), two paintbrushes, a book of Psalms, an advertisement for A NEW SERIAL ROMANCE ENTITLED *NEVER FORGOTTEN* BY THE AUTHOR OF *BELLA DONNA*, some of a bicycle, the blackened head of a puppet (Punch, I think), a darning mushroom, some wild garlic (actually growing on him), parts of two kites (maybe three), the remains of a cat, the bones of a rabbit, many layers of old newspaper, some of a horse, two crucifixes, a length of rubber tubing and part of a door knocker. There were many other things besides, but they had passed beyond recognition. Whatever they were they weren't it any longer.

With each part pulled off, he was growing smaller.

'How do you feel, Mr Tipp?'

'Wrong,' he said, then, 'Wronged.'

I found, how strange the discovery, a patch of skin upon his forehead. I thought it was something else at first, a white tile, something stuck upon him, a bit of rubber. 'Whatever is this?' I asked. 'It won't give!'

'Ow!' he cried.

At last I saw I'd come to the bottom of him, that this was his head, it was not a foreign object. It was his skin, a little patch of it. I leant forward and kissed it. Poor old fellow.

From that patch I went further and scrubbed more, the circle of skin getting bigger. I pulled off a layer or two of old glued bill poster from his face and then some wallpaper (I think) from his nose, there was some stuck tar too, and something that once had teeth, and then it was as if his face was still huge but half the size and there was a person there, frowning back at me, the shock of it. It quite unsettled me, as if now he was wearing the mask, not before. This was someone new, I hadn't known this one earlier.

'Benedict, I think I've found you.'

'Lucy Pennant, I'm lost.'

He leant his mug close to mine and his bruised lips touched mine. Shouldn't call it a kiss exactly. Poor fellow, what ever was that for? He came close again.

'Maybe we shall stop there for now,' I said.

He came forward again, his mouth on mine. That was a kiss, that one. I gave it back a bit, then stopped.

'Well,' I said, confused and in a sudden panic. 'Well, well.'

'Lucy Pennant, Lucy Pennant, what am I?'

'Why, what do you think, you're a man.'

'Am frit.'

'And that's all right.'

'Big frit.'

'Well it's nothing to boast of.'

I put him in some of Mr Heighton's old things, grey trousers, collarless shirt, patched black jacket. There was a pipe in the pocket, that was sad. Poor old Heighton, he wasn't a bad sort, all his poor orphaned objects were still everywhere about the rooms, though by now lacking some of their buttons that Benedict had sought fit to collect. There were boots too, which I struggled to get on him. When he was done he wandered around in the clothing, looking very miserable and only cheered himself up by placing some of the things that had come off him into the jacket pockets, with each added thing weighing him down he seemed a little calmer, a little quieter.

'Well, Mr Tipp, I think it's time we brought you out into society. We're going calling,' I said. 'Mrs Whiting, she's safe, safe as houses. I've known her that long.'

'Don't please not to.'

'You needn't speak much, just say hello and such. I'll do the rest of it, now then, best foot forward.'

He shuffled about, his every footstep bringing noise from the house as it complained under his weight. No one on the stairs, on the landing, very well then and off we went, unto the public. Quite coming out in society.

Up the stairs we went to Mrs Whiting's place. I had been taken on just such a journey as a child, with my parents beside me, exhibiting me to the woman that gave them their jobs. I'd know the place with my eyes out. It had been to me over my life a place of terror, of wonder, of strangeness and possibilities, so full of things as was to me a great delight and caution. Whatever it was I'd be glad enough to see it now. Whatever else it was ever the largest and proudest dwelling in all the house, it was to be found upon the third floor. She had lived there all her life, she had been born there, it was her home. In it she kept mementoes of every stage of her living. She had some of her late parents' hair (carefully embroidered into a pattern and framed), she had her parents' shoes and letters, all her parents' objects. She never threw anything of theirs away.

She was a great respecter of things, Mrs Whiting. She was very proud of her collection. For Mrs Whiting, every object was proof of her living; here was her past all before her, things that confirmed she had been. All sorts of things. The floor of Mrs Whiting's rooms bowed under their weight, indeed her sitting room was a sunken place. Rather than lose any of the weight of her rooms (she would never part with a single object, all was far too precious) she had the Mortons who lived in the flat below turned out and had great steel girders fill their old home to prop hers up.

'Welcome, welcome, Lucy, I so hoped you'd come!' she looked most particularly at Benedict, not trusting him at all.

'Tell me again, Lucy, what is that with you there?'

'Mr Tipp, Mrs Whiting. Mr Tipp, you see.'

'Well, if you insist, though he shouldn't be my choice of a husband.'

'We are not married, Mrs Whiting. He is a friend.'

'Oh, my dear! I am much relieved. Your dear parents should never have allowed it, and now they are gone, and you are back, I see that I shall have to be your parenting figure. I feel I must collect you, Lucy, though I am not sure about Mr Tipp, indeed I am not. Mr Tipp, do you like things?'

'Do yes,' he managed.

'How very sensible, may I show you some of my things, may I?'

'Do yes,' he repeated.

'You are good. Well then we're quite coming along, aren't we? Perhaps there's more to you than first I thought . . . what a man you are! What muscles! Come, come, sit down, I'll bring them to you.'

I had suspected that this might happen, and was in fact hoping for it, so that as Mrs Whiting introduced so many of her things to Benedict, I might, in helping pass this or that to her, I might find some papers of former tenants and keep them for us.

'Please to pass me that vase over there, shall you, Lucy dear?'

I obliged.

'Most kind,' she said. 'Mr Tipp, this vase is my late husband, Arthur Giddings. Arthur was such a sweet man, very gentle with me, but quite weak of chest. He inhaled a child's milk tooth while sorting out in the heaps one day, he came back most wiggy and within a week was a vase as you see before you. Lucy, Mr Shanks, if you would be so kind.'

The old lady was growing quite tearful with her reminiscing and was now full tilt at it. I handed as requested the heavy-cast iron paper slicer from the dresser.

'Here is Mr Shanks, Mr Tipp, a very sharp one was Mr Shanks, not always gentlemanly, and very heavy when on top of one. Mr Shanks proved to have a most provoking temper under his great oiled moustache. He had hopes to be rather more than he was and when melancholy with gin he should become most foul of mouth and should set me screaming as he went about all my things, all my people here, all my dear dead departed friends and tenants, and, do you know, Mr Tipp, he even trampled upon a couple? Of course I called murder and some of my better tenants came rushing to my aid. I have been aided a great deal in my life, I am not ashamed to admit it. I like to be propped up, I do. You, Mr Tipp, have muscles, don't you? Well then, I was talking of Mr Shanks, he made great dents in my mattress – a dear mattress, formerly my great aunt Grace, a most commodious lady in her day – and then one morning, just a night after one of his awful seizures, I wake and there beside me, was that heavy thing! Mr Shanks turned paper slicer. He's dreadful sharp, careful how you handle him!'

Without invitation I next brought to the gabbing old dear Mr Whiting, her pride and joy.

'But Mr Whiting – quite right, Lucy, how I've missed you – was a very different sort of case indeed. I cannot help but grow melancholy when I think of him. Despite all my friends so thick about me, I have felt loneliness since Mr Whiting became a handbell. He was the gentlest of men, not talkative, perhaps. But so few words that are spoken are actually worth the effort, don't you find? Whiting, dear Whiting, he was a whisperer. He used to be one of my tenants, as did Giddings and Shanks before him. He would come and whisper at my door there, and he should slip little things under, so that I should come to wait for them, little missives, a fried plant of some kind, bits of his own dear hair, anything. He knew how I loved it all, his nail clippings, the sweet fellow, and of course I should collect them up. I have a huge collection of all the old bits of Mr Whiting, I may show you if you like. There was much to Mr Whiting until, one day, I could not find him anywhere, nowhere, not throughout my house, for days and weeks I went looking for him. I listened out for his quiet whispering but he was not to be heard. Oh, dear, where could he be and then, there he was, behind the door where I had not thought to look. There! A handbell! A handbell that I had never seen in my life and yet I knew instantly and intimately. Poor, poor Mr Whiting. First Giddings, then Shanks, finally Whiting. What a luckless lady I am.'

I had found them! Pages of them in a drawer, the papers of her expired tenants, many of whom I used to know, the names were all crossed out in pencil, and written in Mrs Whiting's own spidery hand were the things the poor people had fallen into. I put a couple into my pocket and, returning to the overcrowded sitting room, I heard Mrs Whiting addressing Benedict.

'Dear man,' she said, in conspiratorial tones. 'I know when it is coming. I have never yet been wrong in that. Over years I have watched the faces of my husbands, of my tenants, and

I can see the very first play of the disease upon a face. I know when it is near. Let me tell you, Mr Tipp, let me favour you this, it is coming for Lucy, I see it already about her face. She shall turn. I know she shall. I am sorry for it, most sorry. But tell me, Mr Tipp, may we make a deal, when she turns, as surely she must, when she turns, might I have her please?'

Benedict looked at her, uncomprehending.

'You see, if I could have her,' she continued, 'if I could keep her for myself, I mean to look after her. I even – I knew the moment I saw her – I have the perfect place for her, may I tell you?'

Benedict leant forward.

'When she goes, I shall put her over there, between the soup pot and the candle scissors. That's where she'll go. And may I tell you why? Because those two over there are all that remains of her parents.'

Was that them? Was she telling the truth? Was that poor Mother and Father there? I thought that it might be just as she said. I thought they might very well be them. Oh my mother, oh my father. There was something then, after all, something that belonged to me in the world. There they were. Father. Mother. A soup pot. A pair of candle scissors. They belonged to me.

'If you should let me have Lucy when she was turned then I should have, so to speak, the full set. Indeed, those two look very melancholy without her, don't you think? Let me keep Lucy, and understand I'd polish her nicely, she'd never know dust.'

I'd take them, I'd take them now, yet if I did the old woman would surely call for Rawlings and we should be done with instantly. I could not take them, not yet. I shall come back for you, Mother, Father, I promised myself.

'I hope she shan't be very big,' the old woman was saying. 'Lucy is such a slight thing, but you never can tell, can you? There was a child, a baby, barely a few days old, and she suddenly turned. Now you'd think a baby should be something small and delicate, something very tiny and precious, but no, when this baby turned it turned into that great cooking range over there. It is the very devil of a thing, but still I should never part with it, not for anything. I wonder what she shall be when she turns. In truth, I do not think the wait shall be very long at all.'

'Be a botton,' said Benedict.

'Think so?' she said. 'Who can tell? Now, Mr Tipp, here's what I say, I am not a fool, and know when I may crush a person or not, I have not survived this long time without my clevernesses. Now, my dear man – such muscles – if you do not give me Lucy when she's turned then I shall tell Rawlings of your presence here and Rawlings, you know, he shall do for you.'

'Do for me?'

'Yes, indeed, you see, he doesn't like strange people in the house, he won't have them. He knows all the faces of the house, and yours is not one of them. He had a neighbour arrested just for stepping over the threshold last week. She's been taken in, to the station, no one has seen her since, no one's heard a word. There is to be no rule breaking, you understand, Mr Tipp, none whatsoever, but perhaps I'll take a chance with you, and have Lucy on account. Besides, muscles! And yet . . . and yet . . . I seem to recall something suddenly, Mr Tipp, have we met before?'

'No, mum, no, not.'

'Are you certain? I do feel I know you, I feel I've seen you. Your face is not unknown to me, and yet where can it have been? I seem to remember seeing your face everywhere. On a wall! Yes, that's it, a bill poster! Oh, heavens, oh heapness, oh my things! It cannot be!'

'Whatever is it, Mrs Whiting?' I said, stepping forward.

'You've gone and done it, Lucy, haven't you, you've gone and done it!'

'Done what, Mrs Whiting? Please be calm.'

'You've took him from the heaps, haven't you?'

'Please, Mrs Whiting, you are loud.'

'You've gone and done it!'

'Please.'

'Gone and done it.'

'Done what?'

'It, that's what. It!'

'It?'

'That, that thing, the It!'

'His name is Tipp, Benedict Tipp.'

'Binadit! You let him out!'

'Please now.'

'Let him out and brought him here!'

'You must quieten, Mrs Whiting.'

'To my house, little bitch, my house!'

'You'll bring the police in.'

'How could you, how could you?'

'He's a nice man, Mrs W.,' I said. 'Very wronged.' And as I said that I felt Benedict standing next to me, I felt his great hand reaching out for mine. I held it, that big old hand, I'd not let it go, not for anything.

'You don't understand!' the widow shrieked.

'He's done no harm.'

'He was banished . . . thrown out . . . cast away.'

'And there was no right to do it!'

'Idiot child, foolish, foolish girl. He was thrown out, why was he, why was he, tell me that?'

'I cannot say, for some dumb reason.'

'He was born out there. No one knows who his mother was, no one knows where he came from, not from us I think, but they took him in, here to the town, they should never have done that. Children died, all over, but not him, never him, he gets fatter and fatter. My own child died! My own daughter taken from me! There she is on my mantel, that soap dish was once my child, Nicolette Rose! But he goes on, that pig thing, and eats, they give him foul food not fit for rats and still he eats, he eats and thrives. He's not proper, there's nothing proper about him!'

'He is proper,' I cried. 'He's as proper as any of us!'

'No! No, he's not! The filth always stayed over the wall till he came, but after he came, it got out! It fell over, it lurched like it was an ocean. It came after him, wherever he was put the filth followed him. It would fill houses, the stuff that came after him, one old man drowned on it. So they brought him to Town Square, didn't they, they set him down in the centre and stood back, and in a half hour there blew in a mountain of heap, all after him. So that was that then, they threw him over the wall where he belonged where he should ever have stayed! He was ten years of age then, that should make all of about twenty now. And look at that, that thing may as well be twenty as any age! He'll drown us, don't you see? He'll drown us all! He must go back before all Foulsham is drowned!' She began screaming then. 'Get him out! Get him out! Get him out of my home!'

There was noise below, a bell ringing, someone had entered the front door.

'That shall be Rawling,' the old woman said in her panic, 'come home at last. He must not see you, he must not find the It here. What shall happen if he finds the It here, what will they do to me? Hide, hide, both of you! And the moment, the moment it's safe, I want you out! Both!'

The stairs were creaking as heavy feet came up, and a loud, grating voice sung out,

'I've been sifting! I've been sorting!
Over in the rubbish ground,
I've been sifting! I've been sorting!
Come and see what I have found!

'I've been sifting! I've been sorting!
I have found there much for thee,
I've been sifting! I've been sorting!
Let me in now, come and see!'

'Rawling is coming, coming fast,' cried the old woman. 'We shall all be arrested!'

'Mrs Whiting, please listen,' I said, 'where can we hide?'

'Into the hulk cooking range with you both, and close the door hard and fast, you in one door Lucy, hurry yourself, and that It thing into the other, larger one, hurry now, hurry, he'll be here in a moment.'

It was a very large cooker and even Benedict, bent over and squeezed, could fit inside it. He looked very desperate, and I could just about feel him trembling in the other oven beside of me. There was a tiny hatch in the door where a cook may look in and see how his business was proceeding. I could see through it, I could look out.

There was a knock at the door.

'Come in, Rawling,' said Mrs Whiting, 'where ever have you been?'

Mr Rawling was a white faced, balding man, his head slightly misshapen as if he may have been in an accident at some time, he was dressed in a dark grey boilersuit, the lower half of the legs were covered in dirt.

'What's been doing here?'

'What muscles you have, Mr Rawling, what muscles.'

'There's a deal of filth around the house.'

'Indeed your feet are most uncomfortable,' she said.

'And up the stairs, I see someone's been in Heighton's rooms, what's the cause of that? What's afoot, you sneaking old pomfrit? What's going on here while I'm out? There's villainy here, I know it. And why is all the rubbish all around the entrance of the house? What's it doing there? And who's the one to tidy it? It's me. Me and no one else. No one else to do it. And I don't like it! Someone shall have to pay for it, it shan't be me. Why should I?'

'They've found me,' Benedict whispered. 'Oh, Heaps, Heaps have found me.'

'I had to dig my way in to get here,' Rawling was saying, 'and it seems to be collecting up, to be growing around it, as if the heaps themselves were coming here, deliberate like, were forming a place of gathering. And Gatherings, as you know, aren't legal. I'll have to chop it up before it gets too sure of itself. If it gets big then it'll smack at the house and do it great mischief. It's not allowed. Strictly not. Things and people are not to congregate, the rule is very clear on that. I can't think why it's happening when it's against the law. Speaking of law, now, let's see your papers.'

'Mr Rawling, do you really think that necessary?'

'Is the law, I am to do it. Come now, how do I know you're legal? Let's see. Come, come, old girl, hand over.'

He walked over to Mrs Whiting to collect the paper but as he did, he stopped short suddenly. 'Hello now,' he said, 'what's this? What's going on?'

Small bits of heap, scraps of paper and little slivers of glass from Mr Rawling's boots had come free and were slowly twisting their way towards Benedict.

'What's this?' he said. 'What's going on here?' he asked. And then he hollered, 'Villainy! Seek it out!'

Officers of the Heap Wall

16

IT SHALL NOT HOLD

Heapwall log

Entry 26th January 1876
7 a.m.

Heaps are up. Level's rising, has been some spillage over the wall. Not much unusual about that perhaps except that all the storm seems to be against the wall side and the heaps appear to be massing, so that, if this continue, which is very unlike surely, there is certain to be a flooding of this part of Foulsham, the warning horns have not yet been sounded, but it's wise for us to keep strict notice.

10 a.m.

There are cracks on the wall now, undeniable cracks. I do not think it shall fall, surely it shall not, but the cracks are palpable certainly. I could fit my little finger through one. Not good, not good. We take measures with us by the cracks and write with chalk next to them how wide they are and come back every half hour to see if they are widening. They are.

Heap dangerously high, more has spilled over the top, but the wall does hold for now. Sky calm, why do the heaps rage so?

11 a.m.

I have advised clearing the houses and streets nearest the Heap Wall, but Churls Iremonger, Wall Governor, will not permit it, he says we are to stand our ground whatever else. There's emptying of the heaps further out, I see it now, in the distance, Heap House looks naked over there, less and less heap around it, as if it were being abandoned.

I can even see some of the pipes under now, never seen them before, not since I was a child, when they were first laid down, and to do that they had to make special barriers first. I can fit my fist through the deepest cracks.

The rats, the rats are leaving!

They're coming everywhere about us now, squeezing through some of the cracks, or over the top, everywhere you look, never seen the like, never seen anything like it. More and more and more of them. When will they ever stop? From the height of my wall office, I can see down into Foulsham and the street that goes into the town has turned black with rats on the run. It's been black for more than a half hour now. They're going, all the rats, they're on the run.

Heap level still rising.

12 p.m.

One of the men says that Hawkins was measuring a split in

the Heap Wall when a section of wall come off on him. He's dead now, Hawkins is. We're bracing the wall with everything we can, but I am not certain any more that we can last. I don't think Octaviam's wall will see this day out. Governor Churls says that it shall calm down again soon enough, that it shall not breach, but he himself has left now.

I shall sound the siren, whether I am punished for it or not.

My men may leave the Heap Wall and go to high ground. There are two parties of sorters still unaccounted for, you cannot see them, the heaps spit so. And far, far out, Heap House in the distance – do I see this? Can it be true? – seems to be splitting up.

Heap level still rising.

It will spill I think.

It will spill.

God keep us.

Tom Goldsmith, Mrs Bailey,
Bentley Orford and Helen

17

MY INHERITANCE

Clod Iremonger's narrative continued

The Tailor's Room

This is what a room looks like when the world has forgotten it, the floor thick with dirt and dust. Here hid the Tailor Alexander Erkmann for five long years. I could almost feel him there, as if he were beside me whispering, 'Clod Iremonger, Clod Iremonger, you must stop them, you must. You are the one to do it.'

'I am just Clod,' I said to the room, 'and that's not an awful lot.'

But the Tailor was there no longer, he was lost again in the shape of a letter opener. That room, poor room, was a dead place. I needed to see something else, something other than this room, so thick with Tailor. I opened the filthy curtains. The begrimed windows were impossible to see through. I wiped clean a patch the size of my hand, of clear, clear enough, smudged and smoky glass. I looked out across the grey dullness that was the great smoking factory, a hulk of a place, Bayleaf House. There was no mistaking that place, Bayleaf House itself.

Bayleaf House, where my family was, and not only my family,

'My plug!' I said. 'Oh my plug, my James Henry plug.'

I sat in all the dirt and dust, in all that thick air and wondered what was to become of it all.

How much longer, James Henry? I wondered. What time do we have left, before the creeping illness comes into me? What to do in that time? I must go in, I must go in and find those people and see all that they do. However can I stop Grandfather? I used to think living was a safe thing to do. I shall have to wander over there through those gates of metal, slip in there, just a Clod amount of space, and feel through all that smoke, sniff out Grandfather and my family and stop them. However should they listen to me? They never used to. What's changed that they should now? I've changed, I thought then. I've changed. I shall tell them, it's all gone foul and wrong and must be stopped. I'm Clod, I am, and I mean to stop them.

I sat up, the dust moved around me.

'Battle, old Clod, old fellow?' I whispered.

I sat in the dirt.

'I'd manage better with Lucy beside me, that I know. Battle?'

Just sat there in the dirt.

'Well, I may as well march alone. I am alone after all.'

From somewhere deep in the dust, other voices called through the cobwebs and dirt.

'Someone new,' came a voice.

'Come to help?' asked another.

It was an old broken wicker seat talking to a cracked picture frame.

Other obscure things murmured in the darkness.

'Who's there?'

'Who called?'

'Something new.'

'Oh, how he shines!'

'What life he has.'

'Help us, will you,' something called. 'I was Bentley Orford once, am old split bellows now.'

'I was Helen before ever I was this old crib.'

'Oh, hullo,' I said. 'I do hear you. I am most glad of it.'

'Now, that's proper of him,' said the bellows.

'That's breeding, that is.'

'I'm of bad blood, actually,' I said. 'Though I'm awfully glad of your company.'

'No, come now, you're a bright young man, and kind to talk to old broken bits such as us.'

'What shall we call you?'

'Clod,' I said hopelessly. 'Clod the warrior!'

'Clod the warrior, is it? What's your true name?'

'Tummis had some Coldstream Guards,' I muttered. 'I'll be a soldier in my turn, just you see if I'm not.'

'Clan of Orford am I,' said the proud thing. 'My old dad, dear old fellow, lost in the heaps.'

'I am most sorry to hear it,' I said. 'It is awful dangerous out there.'

'That it is, no doubting.'

'I used to watch it from another attic window,' I said. 'Nearly got heap blindness from watching it so often, back at Heap House.'

'Heap House, says you? Heap House?'

'Yes, I did live there, you know.'

'Did you? Why ever should you do that?'

'I was born there, you see.'

'Not Iremonger are you? Not an Iremonger, we had one of them an old dented flask how we hated him and liked to shout at him and make all a misery for him. But suddenly that flask's here no more. Not an Iremonger, are you, surely not. Not with manners like that.'

'I am, yes, I must say I am, through and through.'

'But you sound so different.'

'Do I? I thank you for that at least.'

'We haven't had new company, not for so long.'

'You may come to me,' I said, 'if you like.'

And out of the dirt and dust, making their own timid tracks, broken bits from the attic came and sat beside me. And so we sat together a while, and felt each of us the better for it. Remembering our histories to one another.

We may have continued happily for some time, but then came a noise from somewhere within the house. I had so completely forgotten that there must be more to this place, I'd thought it only a room, but there were surely rooms and rooms beneath me. That was a cheering thought. What went on in those other places? Were there people down there? Were there lives? And I must admit, tears in my eyes, such happiness, that there was! There was life below, because then

I heard a man singing,

'I've been sifting! I've been sorting!
Over in the rubbish ground,
I've been sifting! I've been sorting!
Come and see what I have found!

'I've been sifting! I've been sorting!
I have found there much for thee,
I've been sifting! I've been sorting!
Let me in now, come and see!'

But on hearing this man's singing all the heap bits around me, and on my lap, began to stir again and to retreat into the soft corners, to lose themselves in cobwebs.

'Come back,' I said. 'Please come back.' But they would not, as if they were afraid.

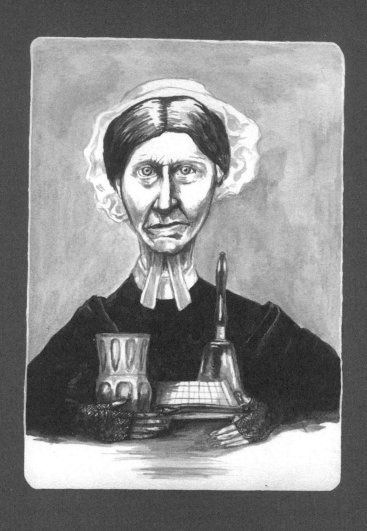

Mrs Whiting and her late husbands
Mr Giddings, Mr Shanks and Mr Whiting

18

IN A COOKER LOCKED

Lucy Pennant's narrative continued

'Binadit,' said Benedict from his place in the cooker.

Please, please, I thought, you must be quiet, Benedict. But the heap bits falling from the cuffs and feet of the new porter were rushing across the floor towards him, and pinging against the door of the cooker, eager to get in.

'What's going on?' asked Porter Rawling. 'What's the size of it?'

The bits stuck fast to the cooker door, like magnets.

'What's the meaning on it, Whiting?' asked Rawling of the old woman, coming closer. 'What have you done, you old sack of bones? You've no license for such a business, this I know. That shouldn't happen, it's against the rules. Why do them things do that? They oughtn't to, I'll have them impounded for less. Hi there, get off that, will you?'

He poked at the things, but the bits stuck fast to the cooker.

'Why would they do that, isn't natural, is it?'

'I cannot tell what you are making such a fuss about,' said the widow. 'Do you not have duties, Rawling? Do not let me detain you further.'

'Is there someone in there, Mrs Whiting, is there now?'

'Rawling, are you insinuating that I am hiding someone in my apartment?'

'That's about the size of it.'

'I am shocked and I am hurt and I am disappointed.'

'Well, well, I can live with that, that's as nothing.'

'I've a headache. I need to be left alone.'

'I've a headache, name on it: Leonora Whiting.'

The porter had his hand on the cooker latch then. 'Who's in there? Come out, shall you?'

Benedict was silent inside.

'You see, Rawling, it is quite empty. How could it be otherwise?'

But Rawling, he lifted the latch, he lifted the latch and he opened the door. He sprung back of a sudden and screamed,

'Well then, look what's for dinner!'

'Binadit!' cried Benedict. 'Binadit! Binadit!'

'What's your name then?' asked Rawling.

'Help! Murder!' cried Mrs Whiting. 'There's a man in my room! Muscles!'

'Come you out,' said Rawling. 'Come you out now, come, come!'

'I stuck,' said poor Benedict.

'Papers!' snapped Rawlings. 'I'll have papers, I will! Papers for being in this house, papers for hiding in that there cooker.

Is it legal, is it right? Get out, get out will you!'

'I stuck cannot!'

'No, no! I'll not sanction it,' the porter went on. 'This is wrong, this is most wrong and I do hate it! I will have order in this house. I am the rule book on these premises, and you, you there, big fellow in the stove, I'm taking you down. You're cooked!'

Saying that, Rawling, in one excited leap, took hold of Mr Whiting and rung him like his life depended on it. That set Mrs Whiting screaming for her husband the handbell and Benedict screaming as loud as he might for 'Lucy Pennant! Lucy Pennant!'

I struggled to get from my portion of the cooker. I struggled to free me. I pushed on the door with my feet but it would not come open. Mrs Whiting had closed the latch and I couldn't get out. I thought we had a chance of getting him, I thought together we could surely overpower the porter, but I could not get free. I could not shift to tell Benedict. He was too confused, the great big man, he needed instruction. And still the porter rang his bell, not stopping for a moment, as if he was not a man at all, only a machine built for the single purpose of ringing a handbell. It all happened so fast. It all went wrong so quick. And then there were other people in the room, men in policing leathers and with truncheons and pikes.

'What is the meaning of it?' called one officer. 'Who are you to disturb the day in this manner? There had better be call for it, better be good call or there'll be such an answering.'

'You,' said another officer to the porter, 'have even interrupted Umbitt with your noising!'

'Umbitt!' cried the porter, most terrified, 'Not Umbitt! Surely not!'

'Umbitt himself!' repeated the officer.

'Oh Umbitt, Owner,' cowered the porter.

'Silence! You little dirtpile!'

'Oh my Maker!' Rawling added involuntarily. 'Didn't mean it.'

'You're making foul noise with that brass instrument.'

'Poor Mr Whiting, dear Mr Whiting!' wept the widow.

'Will you turn that noise off!' said the officer, meaning the widow.

'Shut it, Whiting,' said Rawling, 'or I reckon I'll bash you.'

'What's that then?' said an other officer pointing at Benedict.

'That's what the noise is for,' said Rawling. 'That's a varmint, a walloping great varmint, I reckon. Something huge and unsavoury.'

'Not peculiar to these premises?'

'Most peculiar, but not our peculiar,' said the porter.

'Name, Peculiar, what 'tis?'

'Binadit,' he stammered.

'Name, Binadit? Binadit, did you say?'

'No, no,' poor Benedict stammered, ''tis . . . Benedict Tipp.'

'Why mention Binadit, Mr Tipp? Why would you say that name?'

'No, no, not to mention.'

'How came you here, Mr Tipp?' asked an officer.

'That's the question, let him answer that,' added the porter.

'Shut it, you, stand down, or I'll clock you good and hard.'

'Sir,' nodded the porter, 'sir.'

'Now then, Mr Tipp, explain yourself.'

I kicked at the door.

Benedict stood in front of it.

'I am Mr Tipp,' he said, 'very new here, no home, no lodging.'

'Very like,' said the officer, 'and so you come here of your own volition?'

'I come,' continued poor, poor Benedict, 'for shelter, I come for light, I come for company, I come for the red company that I like so, the red heat, I mean, the warmth, I mean, and I come on my own.'

'Where've you been then, afore you was here?'

'Lost in darkness, Heap! Heap!'

'On the heaps?'

I kicked the door.

'What was that?'

'Was me!' cried Benedict. 'Was my fault, things follow me, things noise for me, I cannot help it. I came here to escape the Heaps, the Heaps were following me.'

'That is true,' said Rawling, 'that's true enough, certainly. I seen it.'

'If I hear you ever once more, Porter, you'll be portering out where no one shall ever hear you and there you may talk till you're blue all over, or any other colour!'

'Sir, sir.'

'Now then,' the officer said to Benedict, 'show me.'

I kicked the door as hard as I could.

'I made the noise,' said Benedict. 'I would like to say, I shall step away and the noise shall not start again, for there's no point in both drowning when one may be safe to help the other later, is there.'

'What are you talking about?'

'I'm telling the stove to be quiet, or I'll be hurt by it, I mean I'll hurt it, I mean it'll be hurt.'

'I'm not following.'

'You see,' said Benedict, leaving me, though it was my fault, all my fault, 'I've been most looked after, I'm happy for it. Now, I shall step away from this thing and when I does it shall be silent, and then, all them heap bits yonder, shall in a moment come along a me.'

I did not kick, I did not call out. I'd raise an army, I bloody would.

'Look, after me,' he said, 'things, oh things, here, come to me.'

I heard one or two of the heap bits following him. 'See how they come after,' he called. 'Come, come, here I be!'

More followed him, more joined into him, covering him over again.

'Come! Come!' he cried and as he wailed, with laughter and horror, the filth from the heaps dragged after him, but he was at the door already, he was out of Mrs Whiting's room and thundering down the stairs before the officers knew what was happening.

'Good God!'

'Did you see that, the things rushing?'

'It's . . . it's It, the Baby, it's out of the heaps.'

'I thought it a story. One to scare the dumb people.'

'Does that look like a story?' the other replied. 'Does the house wobble on account of a story?'

'Must get him!'

'Get him fast, trap him!'

'Call every man! Now, quick, before the walls fall!'

'After him!'

'After him!'

And all ran after, even the porter. What sounds down the boarding house stairs, what calls and hollering. Benedict would outrun them, surely he would, he had a chance, he had a head start.

I called out to the widow then, she was sitting, panting in her armchair with a doily at its headrest, she had her handbell in her lap.

'Mrs Whiting, Mrs Whiting,' I whispered, 'you can let me out now. It's safe I think.'

But she sat on in her chair, stroking her handbell.

'Mrs Whiting,' I said, 'do you hear me?'

'My heart,' she said, 'old organ. Old muscle.'

'Will you let me out?'

'Will I?'

'Yes, will you, please, Mrs Whiting.'

'Oh, Lucy, dear Lucy, I do not think I can.'

'Yes, you can, Mrs Whiting, yes you will.'

'No, no I cannot, you see, dear Lucy, I know that you are about to turn, I've seen it in your face. I do know when such things are about to happen. I've never yet been wrong.'

'Please, Mrs Whiting, I'm begging you.'

'I don't think it'll be very long, dear. Not long at all.'

'I need to get out, please, please Mrs Whiting, poor Benedict!'

'And then all will be done.'

'I have money.'

'Yes dear, but it's not really money I care for.'

'I'll find you such things, better things, the best.'

'I'm so sorry, Lucy, believe me, I am, but I mean to collect you. Do you see? I mean to put you upon the shelf there. I would like that, I'll look after you, have no fear of that. I mean to polish you, and dust you. I shall not ever forget you. I'll cherish you, I promise. You'll never be neglected, but loved, dear, only loved.'

I sat hunched in the darkness, sometimes looking at the old woman through the hatch slit, she dozed with the handbell in her lap. I saw her get up after a while and move her things about, admiring her collection, making much fuss of it, I believe she was readying it for a new member. She was waiting for me. Did I feel like I was turning, did I feel it, that buckling, shrinking, sickening feel? I wasn't certain. The pain in my limbs may just be from my old wounds, or because I was so buckled over in there, the bad feeling in my stomach, that hollow yearning, was surely because I was hungry, because I needed to eat.

Or was it that other pain? Was I beginning . . . No, no, Lucy, you cannot think like that, you mustn't. You've got things to do. You must help Benedict before he's harmed. You cannot turn to a button when he needs you, that'd be no good, how can you help anyone when you're a button . . . a button . . . a clay button. And having these thoughts, round and rounding in my tired head, I seemed to be nodding off. I seemed to be sleeping a while and in that sleep, all of a sudden, there she was. The woman. The matchstick woman, she was very close to me, I knew it. She somehow knew where I was. She sensed it, she sniffed me.

230

'Me,' she said, 'me, me! I come!'

In my dream I tried to run from her, but suddenly there was smoke rising all about and I was choking and there were flames. I dreamt round and round, and felt myself spinning and clattering, growing so small again, and that face, the face of the other woman, long and thin and crying out for her life, trying to take mine from me, to scrabble back. But then suddenly pushing her away was Clod, Clod in a room, in a dark grey room, and the matchwoman was very frightened of him and then she was gone again, the flame was out, the smoke disappeared.

I opened my eyes.

I was still there, locked up in the old woman's cooking stove, still doubled up in the dark, Mrs Whiting was shuffling nearby.

'You're done, I reckon,' she said, 'poor dear. I heard the turning, the fuss, the swift movement, you cannot stop it. I knew you were mine from the moment I saw you at the door. I knew I'd collect you. But you'll be hot yet, I'll leave you to cool a moment. I'm glad it's over; I never like the wait. My poor heart.'

She had a pair of fire tongs with her, she leant them against the cooker.

There was a knock at the door.

'I'm busy,' she said, then she whispered to me, 'This is our moment, isn't it, no one else's?'

She lifted the latch but did not open it.

'Let it cool, best to let it cool.'

I readied myself, put my feet to the door meaning to slam it hard and knock the old bat over.

But instead the door to her apartment was opened.

Hold on, Lucy, not yet, not yet.

'I said I was busy,' said the widow.

There were official Iremonger men walking into the room.

'Good evening, masters,' she said. 'I did not know it was you, I'm very glad to receive you. May I help you, poor old thing that I am, in any way?'

'Your house is in front of ours.'

'I know,' she said, 'that has always been true.'

'It is directly in front of Bayleaf House, the nearest habitation.'

'I have ever been grateful for the view.'

'The heaps are shifting, they are brewing bad.'

'They will get agitated, but if you have put the It back, and I'm sure you have, such capability – muscles! – then it shall calm soon enough. (I know nothing about it, you understand, nothing to do with me.) For myself, I'm an old woman only, thrice widowed with all her small property about her. Little keepsakes, mementoes, of no monetary value, but valued highly, on an emotional plane.'

'Never seen the heaps so upset. And your home so close to ours.'

'We shall, we residents here,' she said, 'under my guidance, keep ourselves most quiet and discreet, a nice house on a nice street.'

'No'

'No?'

'This house is too close by half.'

'It has ever been here, masters, why does it offend you now?'

'There are other movements, movements of people not

houses, there are changes coming, great and fearful changes, changes in which small people, little people, minor creatures, such as yourself . . .'

'Father was tall, I remember.'

'Will likely be brushed aside, trodden on, it cannot be helped. It is the nature of the times. The Heap Wall is buckling.'

'Buckling?'

'It may break.'

'Oh my weak heart.'

'Here we are on high ground, on the highest ground of Foulsham.'

'Are we? *Are* we? Yes, I suppose we are.'

'The great house, Heap House, is uncertain in this weather, and it has been made necessary for some of its residents to be repatriated.'

'Oh yes?'

'To be in a safer place, you understand.'

'Oh yes?'

'They have been moved.'

'Oh yes?'

'The family shall stay in Bayleaf House.'

'Oh yes?'

'And the servants.'

'Yes?'

'They are here.'

'Here in Foulsham?'

'Here in this boarding house.'

'But there are no rooms.'

'There are many rooms.'

'But the paying guests?'

'Are requested to find alternative accommodations.'

'Oh. Oh?'

'You have a question?'

'And I myself?'

'Are to leave.'

'To leave!'

What a scream followed, a scream of a terrible hurt beast, a soul's scream.

'Leave, I cannot leave! Cruel!' she cried. 'This is my home! These are my things! How can I leave them? No, no, it's unthinkable!'

'It was your home, and now it is requisitioned. Take what you can manage and be a history.'

'No! *No!*' she shrieked. 'I cannot! My home! My things! They are *mine*!'

The widow ran around in a panic until she was picked up and carried out, how she cried, the poor old thing, how she scratched at the strong arms taking her away. 'Muscles!' It was enough to make you pity her. I should even perhaps have thought of helping her, only then the new resident of that busy room marched in and I felt all my hope fading away. For I knew her, oh I knew her all right, her in her corset, her with her sharp looks. When she smiled the teeth were quite worn away, I knew that, I remembered that.

Mrs Piggott, housekeeper.

'This,' she said, 'this is my parlour?'

'Yes, Mrs Piggott, until the House has been declared safe.'

'I shall have these ugly things removed, thrown from the

windows, that shall be the quickest way. Let us make short work of it. Iremongers!' she called. Various serving girls ran forward. I knew their uniform, didn't I. Hadn't I worn it myself? 'I'll have a bed set up here, and I want all of this rubbish, every last bit, removed. Do it, please, we'll have this temporary house in order!'

'Yes, Mrs Piggott,' they chorused, they tugged down the windows and let the Foulsham smog in, very thick it was, I could hear the Heaps bubbling and cracking in the background. The servants started throwing out all the precious belongings of Mrs Whiting, they hurled them out into the street below, I could hear them shattering, and along with them, a part of that rash removal, was a soup pot and a pair of candle scissors, my own dear mother and father, and I could not cry out to stop them. And then I saw the faces of those serving girls, many of them I could remember so clearly. I had slept in the same dormitory as them, told them my story, and all of them, to my head were only ever called Iremonger.

But, hang on a moment, that wasn't exactly true either, was it? Not all of them, I knew a name of one of them. Wasn't likely to forget that. There she was, the auburn creature, Mary Staggs herself. I could of spat. How I should like to toss *her* from a high window. With what diligence did she throw the stuff from the old woman's home.

'Wait!' Piggott called. 'Leave that.' She was pointing at Mr Whiting. 'That shall have a use.'

And she put old Mr Whiting to immediate use, her bony wrist flapped back and forth and set the maids all over the house come running to her.

'Listen now, listen good, my dear ones! My Lady Ommaball Oliff is this moment on the train heading towards Bayleaf House, her marble mantelpiece, at great labour, has been uprooted and is in the car beside her. She is apt to be very put out and disturbed. She has never yet spent a day outside of Heap House, nor even out of her own fine apartment. She may be a little short of temper, and we must calm her and be a cushion for her pain, we must provide her with every comfort. There shall be plenty of time to get our quarters ready, right now it is my lady who we must attend to. I want every one of you to be immaculate and lined up upon the station platform ready to receive her. Do you hear me, Iremongers?'

And the resulting resounding, 'Yes, Mrs Piggot!' might have swung chandeliers, had the boarding house any such thing.

Then the serving girls were busy about their business. I saw the unfortunate spectacle of Piggott regarding herself in a small looking glass and picking at her stubby teeth, before at last she smoothed down the corset over her dress and marched out, closing the door behind her.

This was my chance, maybe there shouldn't be another. I'd get out of this house and fast as I could before those Iremongers found me. This house was indeed a deathtrap now.

I pushed open the cooker, it creaked somewhat but no one came. I moved over to the door and looked through the keyhole, no one there, noise down below, no doubt the serving maids were rushing across the way to old Bayleaf House. I'd been in there once myself, before the whole terror began. Well then, give them a moment, clattering on the stairs. No doubt all Sturridge's men were there as well. Wait, wait, don't mess it up, take your time. Listen out. Nothing there? Nothing, all gone out.

So I opened the door slowly, slowly. Come on, Lucy Pennant, out you go, back out, steady, steady.

I was on the landing, no one there at first, not a person, but then suddenly at the bottom, there was Rawling the porter and before him came the heavy thudding of Mr Sturridge and many men in leathers too, their faces quite concealed, all hurrying up, coming my way.

There was nowhere to go, couldn't go back, must go up, up higher, up to the top if needs be, to the very attic. I went up a flight, terrified to see someone on my way, no one yet, a door opened and there was Mr Briggs, the shining underbutler, his door wide open, carefully positioning what looked like a load of pin cushions.

'Briggs! Briggs, man!' called Sturridge.

Briggs dropped a pin cushion in surprise and the moment he bent down to pick it up I rushed past his door and went further upwards, more noise more people in this house, how ever many were there now, up and up, round the corner.

Here, where the carpet was a different colour, grey because of all the dust and dirt, all the cobwebs and dead things, further up, further up, the stairs creaking, shouldn't go up there, wrong to do, my mother said I never should, but I did then, I must, was at the top even, very dark, more noises below, there was a door before me, there was a door handle, I turned it. It wasn't locked, I opened the door, hard to open, pushed hard against, I heard a ripping, a tumbling of stuff, but it gave way at last and I stepped in. Shoved the door closed behind me.

Couldn't see anything, nothing at all, dark, dark.

There's no one here at all, never has been.

But wait.

I felt a coldness against my face.

'Who's there?' I asked.

No answer.

Nothing, no one, spooking myself. That's all.

Was I?

Hang on, hang on just a minute. Go, Lucy, get out, get out of there fast, go down the stairs, run screaming down the stairs, better be out of there, better be anywhere than here, I've been frightened of this place all my life. It's horrid, horrible, something foul's in here, something very nasty.

What was that? Something moved.

I heard it then, I definitely did, something breathing, something in the corner there, something creeping something ghastly. What ever is this foul thing? Whatever it is, it's done bad things. It's all bad, black dripping bad, surely even Piggott had some kindness in her, some little, little good somewhere about? Something breathing there, oh God.

'Who's there?' I whispered.

I heard the breathing more clearly, someone breathing. Someone shifting, in the darkness, coming closer.

'I'm not frightened, come close and I'll give you such a wallop.'

But it came on and it kept on coming.

I wasn't going to let it just chew me up. I wasn't going to walk down its mouth. No, I was going to smack it hard just as it was going to eat me up. I was going to hurt it back, hurt it for all it was worth. I'm Lucy Bloody Pennant I am and I'm that done with hiding.

I let out a gasp and rushed at the thing. I swung a hard thump at its head, what a wallop, and the thing fell to the ground. I'd smacked it good and proper. Hah! What a one you are, Lucy! I'd pulverise the very devil. Come on again, you thing of dark. I'll have at you again. Come closer, I order you, come on up, come another. I'm ready. But the thing, that thing in the corner, it gives out a groan. Kick it, Lucy, kick it, kick it, kick it until it stops, but then it groaned,

'Lucy?'

'Come again?'

'Lucy.'

'What?'

'Lucy.'

'Eh? What?'

'Lucy!'

Clod bloody Clod bloody Clod bloody Clod!

The Porter Rawling

19

OH MY RED

Clod Iremonger's narrative continued

Oh my Red

She hit me. She hit me so hard across the face that truly I thought I might crack like an egg. She hit me, of course she did. How should I know it was her if she hadn't hit me? What a hurt she was, Lucy Pennant, the very best hurt that ever there was.

'Clod? Bloody Clod?'

'Ow!'

'Clod, Clod, say something. Say something this instant.'

'That hurt!'

'Oh Clod, I done it again, ain't I?'

And she was laughing and crying all at once. Lucy was, Lucy again, could she be, could it, how to believe such a thing. Lucy. Lucy. She was kissing me then all over my face, even where it hurt so, kissing and kissing. Her lips found mine. My heavens.

Salty. The warmth of her and the taste of her, there it was again, I'd never forget that. The gladness of it, the giddiness, the joy. Such joy. That feeling in me, building.

'Lucy?'

'Yes it bloody is.'

'I never thought I'd see you again.'

'And there's faith for you, right there.'

'And Lucy you're not a button.'

'Can a button do this?' she said, kissing me. 'And this?'

'I do not believe so. Perhaps you may try again?'

'I've been a button,' she said. 'I was nearly a button not long ago, and she means me to be a button again. Ada Cruickshanks does.'

'And I've been thinged, Lucy. I've been a golden half sovereign in my time since last I saw you,' I said.

'Have you?' she laughed. 'Isn't that just like you. I have to be a clay button and you get to be a sov. Where's your plug then?'

'I've lost him. And your matches are still with them?'

'They're somewhere close by, that's for certain, I can feel her, very near she is. Looking for me, you might say. Sniffing for me.'

'Then we're both likely to be very ill, I think.'

'Well, I shan't be a button again. I shan't let her. I'll get her goat.'

'Lucy, Lucy Pennant, it's you and your considerable red hair and all your freckles.'

'Every one of them!'

'I am right glad.'

"Right glad' are you? I'd forgotten how posh you are.'

'Oh Lucy, there's much to do, and terrible business it is.'

'Know where we are, Clod? This minute?'

'Foulsham . . . and out of the window, I saw just through the curtains, is Bayleaf House.'

'And what are we in? Name on this particular location?'

'I do not know it, a poor place of some sort.'

'Careful now, I'll knock the other side of you. It's my home, isn't it, where I grew up.'

'Is it? How strange. I should like to see it, could you show me?'

'Not just yet, there's people below with dreadful bad manners. They'd like to have us, no doubt, be most grateful to know that we're up here all along.'

I told her of my run through Foulsham and of the Tailor. But most of all of the business of Bayleaf House, of the breathing in of childhoods.

''Tis monstrous. I'll kill them Iremongers! 'Tisn't right! To do that!'

'I'm an Iremonger, I'll always be an Iremonger.'

'And I'm a Pennant, last there is. Can't help your family, they say, can chose your friends. You, you're my friend, I chose you. There, live with it! I've been searching for you, I made a promise, you're stuck with me, Clod Iremonger, I'm your thing. Like it, lump it, don't make much difference, you're in my heart and there's an end on it.'

'Lucy, I must stop all this.'

'Not without me. I won't let you.'

'This is all Iremonger doing.'

'I'll give you such a knock.'

'Oh, Lucy, I am so happy to see you, at least there's you for all the pain. When did you come to yourself again, however did you manage it?'

And she told me all that had happened until the moment she opened the attic door and found me with a thump. And there was something terrible in that story, something to break my heart and stop anything from coming right ever again.

'You kissed him?' I asked.

'Well, he was the one that done it really,' she said. 'I was just there.'

'But you didn't push him away.'

'Well,' she said, 'no.'

'Oh.'

'Come on, Clod, don't go quiet on me. You're the talker you are, you never stop talking.'

But I did not feel like talking then. I felt my Iremonger heart shrivelling up, growing smaller and harder.

'Come, Clod, it didn't mean anything.'

Smaller, smaller.

'Clod, talk to me.'

'Do you love him?'

'Oh, Clod!'

'If you love him,' I said, 'I shan't stand in your way.'

'What a child you are!'

'No doubt.'

'Clod, dear Clod. I shouldn't have told you. I just wanted to tell you everything . . . Clod, Clod!'

'I'm going now,' I said, getting up. 'I've business to attend to.'

'Clod!'

'What's that?'

We both were suddenly very quiet then, we both had heard it. There was someone on the stairs.

What are Little Men Made of?

Whoever it was was coming slowly up the attic stairs, whoever it was didn't stop but came on. We both kept very still. A scratching voice quietly sung out,

'I've been sifting! I've been sorting!
I've been gone so very long,
I've been sifting! I've been sorting!
Come and harken to my song!'

The singing stopped. Started again.

'I've been sifting! I've been sorting!
I am coming now to you,
I've been sifting! I've been sorting!
I am here now! Here now! Boo!'

'Who's there?' the someone the other side of the door asked. 'Whoever is it there? I do know there's someone. I heard voices. I've not heard voices before, not until this day. Is it one of the new servants, don't be afrit if it is. There's nothing to be frit of. It's only me, Rawling the porter. I'm going to open this door now; I'm a-coming in.'

The doorhandle turned, the door was heaved open. There was a dark figure there, stumbling blindly in the half-light.

'Who's there?' he called. 'I'll know you if you please.'

I listened to him, listened for his inner voice, but there wasn't one, nothing at all. He was absolutely silent. There was no noise, no sound, no mutter from within him, just an emptiness there, a hollowness, nothing, no one, no man.

'Who's there?' he called once more, but his voice was breathless now, like he was frightened. 'I know you're in here. Come out will you? I'll not be angry.'

I heard the things of the attic creeping away, trying to get away from him.

It was the opposite of the gathering that pursued me across the Forest of the Roof of Heap House, that thing made more noise almost than the heaps, but this thing was silence itself, no sound came out of it. I'd never heard such empty silence.

'Come now, let's be having you.'

He was close to Lucy, edging in her direction. He had no right to do that, not this thing, not this no-noise, this quietness. I would not let him touch her, I would not let him.

'You're not anyone,' I said.

'Who said that?' cried the man-thing Rawling, turning in my direction. 'Come here now. I'll have you now. I know where you are.'

'You're no one, are you?' I said.

'Papers, I'll have papers.'

'But what about *your* papers?' I said. 'Whatever name they have on them is a lie, you're not real.'

'I am,' he said, offended, put out, as if I'd stung him. 'I'll show you how real I am. Come here, you varmint!'

'You're no one, Mr Rawling.' This was from Lucy, in another part of the room, following on from what I was saying, playing my game. Rawling spun around. Lucy said, 'You're not anyone at all.'

'There's two on them!'

'Here I am,' I said.

'Here I am,' said Lucy.

'Here I am,' I said.

'Here I am,' said Lucy.

He swung for Lucy and had hold of her by a wrist.

'Well then, I got one of you, haven't I?'

I rushed over, I felt in the half-light for the buttons around Rawling's thick suit. I found one, two, I pulled them open, ripped them off.

'Here!' he cried. 'What's happening? What are you doing?'

He thrashed out, he struck me and I fell.

'Lucy,' I said, and I prayed I was right. 'I've undone two of his jacket buttons. Listen to me, you must rip him open. He's not real, he just seems it. He's not an actual person; he's just made of bits. Feel for the stitching.'

The man Rawling snapped his jaw like a dog, snapped it closer and closer to Lucy's face.

I called then, to the broken bellows, the old picture frame, to the crib.

'Now, I do beg you, Bentley Orford, Helen, Mrs Bailey, I do beg you now. I hear you over there, Tom Goldsmith. I do hear you. You're a wicker chair, I know. I do beg you, come at him, come at it, or he'll so pull the life out of everything.'

Nothing, no movement, and Lucy struggling.

'I do command thee!' I cried.

'Clod!' cried Lucy.

'Varmint!' cried the porter.

'NOW!' I bellowed.

And then they swooped, and then they came raining in.

'Lucy, down, get down!'

The chair came behind him and kicked him like a horse he fell into it, and it, dear Tom Goldsmith, lacking any wicker seating, caused the porter to sit down trapped. Then the old crib flew from the corner and smacked his head, so that it knocked right back, and should have stopped any true man, but the head swung back and the face, though horribly squashed, was still there and re-forming.

'Here!' he cried. 'What are you doing? 'Tisn't legal, is it?'

Then swooping down like some albatross came Bentley Orford the split bellows and it dived into the trapped stomach of the porter and it punctured a good hole, and then up it climbed, flying round to come at him again.

Once there was an opening the rest was easier, I ran forward then and pulled at it, made a great huge rent, such a tearing. It was as if someone had ripped a bit of the world.

'What?' he said, quite stunned. 'What have you done to me?'

I opened the curtain, let in the light. There was this man Rawling sat in the middle of the room, Lucy in shock, backing away from him. There was a great hole in his shirt, only it wasn't a him, and pebbles and bits of old glass and sand were pouring out of it onto the floor.

'You didn't ought to do that,' he said, as it tumbled out. He tried to stop it, he caught some in his hands, but the rest poured on.

'You're not anyone,' I said to him, calmly as I could.

'I'm Rawling,' he said, but even as he said it his head was sinking in like a sack being emptied.

'You're not a person,' I said. 'You're not. I'm sorry.'

'Oh,' he, *it* is more correct, it muttered.

'Oh . . . oh . . . oh I didn't know,' it managed.

The rest of it fell down just then, an old leather thing, tipping out. Out came the stench again and a small cloud of black air, fading on the attic ceiling. Not human, how ever had we thought it was? And then it had stopped, it was just a pile of emptied stuff, a burst something or other.

'What was that?' said Lucy.

'It was just things put together and stitched up and given a little warmth,' I said. 'It didn't have a noise within it, there was no sound. I couldn't hear anything coming out of it, nothing at all. Just silence. Awful silence.'

We looked down at the strange puddle that was Rawling, his leather skin all hollowed out.

'How, Clod, how did you do that, move all those things about?'

'Yes, Lucy, I had almost forgot. Go now, go quick, Tom and Bentley, Mrs Bailey and Helen, quick now, up the chimney and out of the attic, to newer homes. I do thank. I thank you.'

Some tumbled down the stairs, the bellows smashed right through a window.

'What a business,' Lucy said. 'To do that! Clod, little Clod, what a thing! What a person you are!' she said, but she looked shocked at me, disturbed, I might say.

249

'Yes,' I said, after a moment, 'I think it was well done.'

'That took some doing, opening him up like that.'

'Oh Lucy, he was so silent.'

'Wouldn't do to make a mistake, would it? To undo a man . . . who wasn't made of muck.'

'No, no indeed I do not think it should.'

'Clod?'

'Lucy?'

'Clod?'

'Lucy?'

'Clod, I'm sorry, Clod. Oh Clod, it is you, whatever it is that you can do, still is after all only you. Oh Clod, listen, it was nothing, that bloody kiss. You should see the poor creature, he's been in such trouble. And I don't know where he is now, or if he's safe. I think he must go back to the heaps. But only if he wants to, only then. He's so helpless, though so big a fellow. Perhaps we could help him, you and me, we should. Then you'll see him, you'll understand then.'

'Lucy,' I said, 'I think for my part that I must go into Bayleaf House.'

'We can help one another, can't we? We're all we've got, aren't we?'

'I've got to stop Grandfather.'

'Well then, I shall come along too.'

'It is Iremonger business.'

'Is it? Oh, is it? And I've got a box of matches over there through those gates and I mean to have them. So we'll be moving in the same direction I reckon.'

'It's a free world.'

'Not much it isn't.'

'But it *should* be,' I said, 'and that's the point.'

'Perhaps I shall need your particular hearing, Clod, in the search of my matches, perhaps you'd oblige. Maybe you'd set a dinner service on them for me.'

'I hear the undervoice, Lucy, inside everyone,' I said. 'I hear it getting louder when it's going to turn, till it's almost shrieking in my ear. The object sort of calls out, it's not English, but I seem to hear it. It gets louder and stronger and then it sort of gallops in speed and then there's no stopping it, then it flips the person. Past a certain point there's no stopping it, I think.'

'Do you hear it, Clod?' she said, stepping towards me, 'Do you hear it in me? It's not shrieking now is it?'

'No, no, it's not, not now.'

'What an awful queer fellow you are,' she said, stepping closer.

'I'm sorry for it.'

'Not your fault I suppose.'

'Very kind of you.'

'Glad to see you.'

'Yes,' I said, 'most awfully.'

She opened her arms and I went to her, we held each other tight, so tight against everything that surrounded and threatened to bring us down.

'What do you hear?' she said.

'"Clay button",' I said, '"clay button" to the rhythm of your heart.'

Her Royal Highness Victoria
by the Grace of God

20

AN INSTRUCTION TO TERMINATE

Being the official and final proclamation
concerning the Borough of Forlichingham,
London
Highly Secret

WESTMINSTER, LONDON

ON THIS DAY, the 26th January in the year of our Lord 1876,
it has been declared by unanimous vote that the borough
district of the great city of London, Capital of the British
Isles and of the British Empire, that is called by the name
FORLICHINGHAM, is deemed a place of HIGH TOXICITY
and is DANGEROUS UNTO THE HEALTH OF THE
NATION.

Daily reports of deaths by noxious gas escaping from that
region and of a most gross and disturbing build up of *FILTH*

has brought into danger the very existence of London. Two hundred and twelve (212) pensioners of the neighbouring borough of Lambeth have been found stiff and discoloured and dead in their homes. An increase of RICKETS has been noted in INFANCY throughout the CITY. BLACKLUNG is increasing. The infection *VIBRIO CHOLERAE* more commonly termed BLUE DISEASE, believed to have been tamed under the labour of JOSEPH WILLIAM BAZALGETTE, is once more in the INCREASE. Daily the winds shed POLLUTANTS from *FORLICHINGHAM* into the city, and that there is a general air of SWEET FOUL STENCH from the top of HIGHGATE unto the bottom of SHOREDITCH. That this FOUL AIR is POISONING and REDUCES LIFE, and that in the market of COVENT GARDEN it has been shown as PROOF that milk arrived in that place SPOILS WITHIN A HALF HOUR due to the PUTRIFYING STENCH of *FORLICHINGHAM*.

THEREFORE, after great discussion and debate, having sought advice of the great officers of HYGIENE, and of those of understanding of the DISPOSAL OF REFUSE that the place *FORLICHINGHAM*, previously given license unto the family known as *IREMONGER* to take from LONDON all that LONDON discards, is a license that is now, under immediate notice, REVOKED PERPETUALLY. And that, this family *IREMONGER*, no longer to any satisfaction policing the EXPULSIONS of LONDON, that the region *FORLICHINGHAM* is a HORRID and DANGEROUS region, known for FILTH, VICE and MURDERINGS COMMON, that therefore it is deemed MOST necessary that the place *FORLICHINGHAM* be TAMED or REMOVED from LONDON. And that therefore, it is understood that there being no chance of BRINGING CLEAN and CALM such a POISONOUS and POISONING location, that the place *FORLICHINGHAM* be in a most thorough and complete way REMOVED, DESTROYED, BROUGHT DOWN, ERASED, from LONDON, and that LOSS OF LIFE therein of the inhabitants of the (FORMER) borough of *FORLICHINGHAM*, be deemed regrettable but ESSENTIAL for the SURVIVAL of the SOVEREIGN city LONDON.

Therefore in SOLEMNITY do we the below signed agree this day, that the place *FORLICHINGHAM* be in a most SWIFT, THOROUGH, ABSOLUTE and TERRIBLE way, **BURNT UNTO THE GROUND** until the HEAT of FIRE has in COMPLETE STERILITY destroyed all GERMS that there abide.

The actions (being all complete in readiness and preparedness in desperate advance of this bill) to ACHIEVE all the above NECESSITIES be carried out with due SPEED and DILIGENCE.

And that as such, it shall become, in the name of Her Majesty, Victoria, by the Grace of God, of the United Kingdom of Great Britain and Ireland, Queen, Defender of the Faith, Empress of India, immediate

LAW

People of Foulsham

21

TO THE GATES

Lucy Pennant's narrative continued

I called them all leathermen after that, after Porter Rawling
had been unstitched and spilled all over the attic floor. That's
how we always knew them as after, those people, those things
I should say, them leathermen.

Clod told me there were hundreds of them all over Foulsham.
I couldn't say if it were true or not, but Rawling seemed so
realistic that who's to say, really, when you look about, who's to
say who's real and who's not? There are many people over the
years I always thought may just have been filled with sawdust
for all the sense you got out of them, and others too who had
been so cruel and unkind that they may just as well have been
sharp metal through and through, deaf to all bargaining and
pleading. Well then, who's to say who's a person?

He was. He had life in him; he could command things to
move, however should a person do that. Who ever was Clod,

that thing-mover? He looked iller, he shook rather with the weight of it all. I should never have told him about that kiss, should never, that was stupid. I just wanted him, of all people, to know everything about me. Clod with his big old head and his worried eyes, thinner, thinner. No plug about him. His white skin, so white like paper, I'd kiss that all over. Why him, I wondered. Why of all of them, him? Not so very much to look at. You might think that if you didn't know him.

Didn't matter what he looked like, he was himself. He was fighting against it all, my Clod, my everyday Clod. Wouldn't be without him now, not for anything, I'd keep him very close. Never felt that before. All of him. All of me. Can't break something like that, can you? That's strong isn't it? How strong is it, I wondered. Others should try to cut it. Couldn't let them.

I prodded the Rawling pile with my foot.

'Well, Clod, he doesn't look very dangerous now, does he?'

'No, no, Lucy, not one bit.'

'He seemed not to know what he was.'

'I don't suppose they do. I don't suppose any of them do. And there are hundreds of them, Rippit said, they're everywhere about. All Grandfather's dolls.'

'What's he want with them, an old man like that, with his toys?'

'He's building an army,' said Clod. 'That's what the Tailor told me, a great army, to take on London itself.'

Army. That word again. Gnawing at me.

'We'll get us an army and all,' I said.

'Lucy Pennant, how should we ever do that?'

'Nothing will ever be right, will it,' I said, 'not if we don't stand up for it. We live our lives cowering in an attic room until our days are spent. Everyone's hiding in the shadows, being knocked down, one by one, being taken by Umbitt and all his kind. How many hundreds have just sat there and let it all happen to them, all the hunger, selling off their own children? It won't do any more; we'll stand up. We'll not let it go on any longer. We'll have an army of our own. We'll go from street to street, from house to house, and we'll get them to come along with us. We'll show them, and every time we stand up to the Iremongers, then that's a victory, isn't it, and if enough of us stand up and keep standing up then they'll be done for, I reckon. There's more of us than them, much more, if we all get up and say "No" and "Shan't" then that'll hurt them, that'll crush them, shan't it? We'll bloody do it, we'll show them!' I cried. I'd worked myself up, like I was standing at a pulpit but there were only me and Clod, children in an attic room. I'd sort of forgotten that bit, that brung me down a little. 'Well, that's what I think.'

'Yes,' he said softly. 'Yes, I think that too.'

'You do?'

'Yes, Lucy, I'm not afraid to die. I was, was very much in truth, when I was a coin, when I couldn't do anything, only just be moved about by other people, that was frightening because I was lost then, but I'm me again now, and I know Grandfather and what he could do, and I'll do anything to stop him.'

'Then we don't care if we die?'

'No, we don't care if we die.'

'Let them kill us.'

'It'd be just like them.'

'Last time it was for you to show me about, Clod. Now we're on my turf. This is my place isn't it? It may not be as big or grand as yours, but it's not stolen and before your family moved in it was filled with good people. Well it was filled with ordinary people at any rate. They weren't doing anyone any harm, not for the most part. If there's any in this house that still knows me, we'll find them. And we'll get my school fellows along too.'

'Lucy, I do like your idea of an army. It sounds wonderful indeed, and I think of all the people I know you'd be the person to do it, but I think that it should take a time, shouldn't it, and I think there may not be so very much time. Perhaps you may find your friends, will you, and meanwhile I shall go to those gates.'

'Well,' I said, terrified of parting from him, 'well, I could come with you . . .'

'If you could find friends, if you could get help, that should be best I think.'

'Do you? Should it?'

'Lucy, I think if I can get to Grandfather, if I can get hold of his personal cuspidor, Jack Pike is its name, that's what I hear it saying, if I could only get hold of Jack Pike, and steal it from him. Or if only I could make Grandfather stop it all, oh perhaps, perhaps I may have to kill him. Perhaps I may call upon all the objects in there, if I could summon them, perhaps they'd come to me, perhaps they might . . . well, there's no good just talking about it, we must get on.'

'Clod? Clod, would you do such a thing?'

'I could get close, you see. I'm an Iremonger. They'd let me through I think. It does make sense. They don't know that I can ask the things to move, they don't know that yet. So perhaps I may do something with that after all. And it's best not to think of it, overly much, but to rush along, right now. Show me down, Lucy. Get me out of this place. Deliver me to the gates, and then get your friends.'

I didn't say anything to that. If I spoke I knew I'd start weeping. And I mustn't do that. Not a baby am I, after all. Time enough for weeping, Clod, when you're out of my sight.

There wasn't anyone on the landing, not straight off. Most of them had gone across the way into Bayleaf. We'd heard the train arriving, the old woman, that dreadful old woman. Made me sick just to think of her. She'll have come now, must have, the train had made its great shriek.

Looking through a downstairs window there was much running about outside the house. There were crates laid out before the place, all busy, them Iremonger ants, all such a rush on.

We'd made it down one floor, two more to go. There was the old crib on the landing now, beside it the wicker chair. And we were making our steady progress, and couldn't hear anyone nearby, even Clod couldn't hear anyone and that was the best proof of all, wasn't it, because there was never a one for lugs than Clod with all his hidden voices, quite mental when you think about, so on we were creeping in our little way when there came a mighty noise, didn't there. It was a long, wailing, trumpeting sound. I knew that, didn't I? Well enough to make me stop dead in my tracks. I'd heard it before, way back in my childhood when a heapgate came crashing down and fifty people were crushed or drowned.

Should never like to hear that noise, even when it was only sounded for practise, to make sure the great horns were still working. It was the flood horn, one of the great flood horns of the Heap Wall. Where that horn stood there was danger and all must flee from that part, but then there came another horn and another yet, and another, yet another, all joining up, all calling out, all of them, all across the wall. All the horns were sounding, I reckoned, from all over the wall.

'What is it, Lucy, why do you look like that?'

'The walls, Clod. It's the siren for the walls, never heard that many going off at once before. I think the wall may come down, and not just in one place but all over. Oh, I think Benedict is still out then, they have not put him back.'

'And what should happen then, Lucy, if the wall comes down?'

'Then it shall flood, shan't it, you dunce, what d'you think? It'll flood the whole place, it'll all come down. And hundreds, hundreds will be drowned!'

'Is there nowhere safe?'

'This is the high ground here. This is where they'll come. Safer here, but not safe, there's nowhere that's safe if the wall comes down.'

'Everyone will come? All here?'

'Yes, Clod, and soon, any moment, I reckon, all will bubble up around us.'

'I shan't hear, Lucy, I shall not be able to hear anything. I'll be so deaf, it'll be worse than the storming in Heap House, a thousand times worse than that. I shan't be able to hear the objects' names, and without hearing their names I never shall be able to command them.'

'Well then, you'd better keep close, hadn't you?'

'But I think perhaps, it may be, in some small way, perhaps it is good news, Lucy. I think it might be.'

'What's good about it?'

'That's when I'll go in and find Grandfather, in all the chaos.'

'Oh, Clod, are you dumb enough?'

'I think I am.'

There was silence then, a strange long silence between the warning horns and all that followed, like grabbing a little bit of air before plunging deep under the waves. Like the intake of breath before screaming. Small silence, but what a pregnant silence, shouldn't last, shouldn't last.

Then there was a sort of mild buzzing sound in the distance like that of an insect humming about, except the insect wasn't rushing about rooms in the still winter cold, bouncing into windowpanes, no, it was outside, and the buzzing didn't stay on a note, that deep humming grew louder and got greater until you could tell what it was. It was the noise of people all together, not knowing what to do other than scream, and all screaming, all roaring together in a panic, all of one mind. It was a great collection it was. I'd heard of all those other collections before, a parliament of rooks, a squabble of seagulls, a mischief of rats, an itch of Iremongers, well here was another one to add to it, a new collective: a panic of people.

'Everyone's coming?' Clod said.

'A whole army,' I said.

'But you can't control them, can you? They're all in a chaos.'

'Might,' I said, 'might just.'

'Who's there?'

People up the stairs then, coming towards us, three of them, big fellows in leathers, all leathers, hood and all, the works. I looked at Clod.

'Lucy,' he whispered, 'I can't hear anything, except for a button. It's quiet enough now. They're Rawling's sort.'

'What you doing here? This place is requisitioned!'

'Is it?' I said. 'Well no one told us.'

'You're not to be here!'

'Why, who says so?' I asked.

'Umbitt, owner.'

'This is my home. I was born here.'

'Taken over, requisitioned.'

'Oh yes?'

'Most certainly!' the leatherman said.

'Do you hear that noise?' I asked. 'That rising rumbling?'

'We hear it,' they said.

'Know what it is?' I asked.

'Heaps,' they said. 'Heaps is upset.'

'No,' I said, 'it's not the heaps. It's not the heaps at all. It's Foulsham that noise is, all the people of Foulsham, and do you know what they're doing? They're coming up this way, and I think they're unhappy and, you know what, I think they'd all like to come inside, come and live in this high-ground home. They'll break the door down, I reckon.'

Well it wasn't brilliant but it was a start. It was practise, wasn't it, the leathers, dumb creatures, looked at one another and in a mumble hurried away down the stairs in a rush, gone to see for themselves.

Shouldn't be long now, certainly shouldn't, that great noise was smashing around the old buildings of Filching, strange noise to my ears, bouncing off here and there, ugly, distorted, misshapen, that's what it was to my ears, Lord knows what it was to Clod's. We went down after the leathers.

'Where are you going?' they said.

'Out,' I said. 'You told us we weren't to stay here.'

'That's right. Very good. Sling your hook.'

'Good luck,' I said, 'for you shall surely need it.'

'Hey, what's the matter with him? He looks quite turned he does.'

Poor Clod was very white and trembled all over, there must have been that roaring in his head, like all the people of the world at his earholes and shouting in them, not just the voices of them screaming, but the voices *in* them, all a tumble. Couldn't listen to that very long, I supposed, not for long before you'd go mad with all the noise. I had to get him in, into Bayleaf House before all that racket made his brain turn porridge.

'He's all right,' I said to the leathers, 'just sensitive, he's made of silk he is, unlike you lot.'

'Hop it,' said a leatherman, what a look on his face, panic it was. Couldn't blame him really. You could see the crowds now, rushing up hill, they'd be here any moment. Don't want to get between them and those leathers, shouldn't give them the pleasure.

On, Clod, on we go.

269

He looked at me, pointed to his ears, shook his head.

I nodded back at him.

All right then, no more talking, this is it, this is. There it stood, Bayleaf House, its chimneys still spewing, greyer than any grave, hard and cold and unlovely, well then, onwards. Better hurry. That noise behind us was coming on fast.

I tugged us over, up the hill and to the very gate.

Part Three

Bayleaf House Factory

The Grand Officer Moorcus Iremonger
and his Toastrack

22

AT THE GATES

Lucy Pennant's narrative continued

The sentry was closing the factory gate up, locking it.

'Let us in,' I said. 'You must let us in.'

'No entry!' said the sentry. 'Strict orders.'

'Did you not hear the horns sounding?'

'That I did.'

'Know what that means?'

'Likely there'll be a flooding.'

'And people will drown.'

'I can't help that.'

'You'll let people die.'

'I have my orders.'

'Listen, just let us in, before the others come, will you? My friend here, he's not well as you see.'

'No,' he said, 'can't be done.'

'I've some money,' I said.

'I'm not talking to you no more. Disperse.'

'Yes you are talking to me, and you'll keep talking, and you'll let us in. Listen, he's an Iremonger, isn't he. An actual Iremonger. He belongs the other side of the gate.'

'No one's to come through, no exception.'

'He's Clod Iremonger.'

'I don't care who he is.'

'He needs to be let in!'

'No one can pass!'

He stood silent, as other guards ran to the gate, there were more then, ten, twenty of the Iremonger guards with their Bayleaf collars, all running out, a sergeant among them now, wearing a brass helmet, thinking himself very grand no doubt. Then I saw his medal. Something familiar in that. Then I knew him, Moorcus Iremonger, Clod's cousin. He that was the cause of Tummis's drowning. I pushed Clod. What to do? What to do? I saw behind Moorcus then, always nearby, like a dog on a leash, his turned birth object, his Rowland Cullis. He'd help if there was ever a chance, surely he would.

Behind us the first Foulsham people were coming, all in their rags and leathers, holding what things they had, never very much, all that they could carry, maybe all that they owned, children on shoulders and in carts, old people in carts, all the worried, hungry, desperate, all up to the gate of Bayleaf House, with the horns blowing again and all the terror that the Heap Wall was going to give, and all would drown in its bursting.

I didn't need to talk then. We stayed at the gate, we'd be the first through I reckoned. Wouldn't lose our place, not if I could help it. I was pushing them off already. I was standing our ground. Poor Clod looked terrified to his soul. He looked down mostly, wincing all the while, all those people in his head, couldn't keep them there long, and more people coming on, the gates around Bayleaf House thick with people, so many people, all Foulsham at the gates. Moorcus marched forward, he called out,

'You will disperse, no congregations of people are permitted. This is private property.'

'Don't you hear the horns?' someone called.

'There is no danger, there is no cause for alarm. Please disperse now, go back to your homes.'

'But the horns,' another person shouted, 'do you not hear them? They're all sounding!'

'The walls shall hold,' Moorcus said, and how white he looked. 'Nothing can break the great Heap Wall. You are all safe. Go home, please, go home. All is well. Grandfather – Umbitt Owner has issued his guarantee. The wall is safe. Go home. Do not be distressed.'

That stopped many of them, some fell to whispering then, perhaps all was well, perhaps it was safe to go home.

'Move along now,' said Moorcus, 'go back to your homes, get back now. You'd do well to go home, see that your homes are safe. There are looters at large, it has been reported, even now your homes are in peril. Why will you not protect your things? What have you left there? It may not be there when you go back, quick now. While you still have time.'

And that did it for some of them. Those sheep, they trembled and trotted off back down the lane though the horns had sounded. How they cowered. They weren't people, they were beasts of burden. They'd do anything you ever told them. Believe anything if it was said official enough. They'd all drown, they were going back now, turning around, heading down, down to their drownings. But these were my people, my people that I'd lived with all my life, my people who'd been tugged down so much it hurt to get up, they had to stand up, they had to stand up or they'd have no chance. An army, an army, hold fast together.

'He's lying!' I shouted. And some even stopped their plodding right then. 'He's lying! He just wants you to get away. He's sending you away to drown. Do you not hear the horns? Are you deaf? Them horns mean danger, the wall's going to give!'

'Shut it, miss,' said the sentry, 'that's enough!'

Clod looked up at me, he couldn't have heard but he had a pained smile on his face, and that was encouragement enough.

'He's sending you down to your deaths,' I called. 'You want to die, off you go then, trot along. But I'm staying here and if we all stay here, then we'll get through this gate and be on the high ground. If we all stay they can't stop us. How many more of us are there than them?'

'Hundreds. Hundreds on us!' Jenny called from the crowding.

There she was, there was Bug and all, and the rest of the kids from school, all together: there's a voice, I reckoned, there's lungs there. Now's the time.

'How long will we let them break us?' I had such a taste for it then. 'How long must they order and bully? They let us drown out there in the heaps. How many of us have been pulled under? They've taken our children from us, how many of our children are in that building now, stolen from us! What have

278

they done with them? Come now, let us see. We will be let in!'

'Let us in!' called Jenny.

'Let us in!' echoed her schoolfellows.

'Your children have been ticketed,' called Moorcus, so white now, Rowland in the background behind him, smiling, enjoying Moorcus's misery. 'You have been compensated, heavily compensated. Your relations are all well and all cared for.'

'How do you know?' I cried. 'Have you seen them?'

'We haven't,' someone grumbled.

'No, we haven't,' called Jenny.

'That's right,' from somewhere else, the voices coming from all over now, we'd got them talking.

'Look up, good people of Foulsham,' I shouted, my face as red as my hair, 'look up there at that building, our people are in there and beyond this gate is high ground and safe.' Then I chanted, 'LET US IN! LET US IN! LET US IN!'

'LET US IN!' they went.

'LET US IN!'

'LET US IN!'

What a chorus, what a people, what an army.

'People of Foulsham . . .'

'LET US IN!'

'People of Foulsham . . .'

'LET US IN!'

Jenny and her company came around to me then, all that young of Foulsham, such schoolfellows, so strong of voice, all busy about me, all flared up for the fight. Moorcus's hands were shaking. He held a shining pistol out. He fired it into the air. The people moved back a little, so many hundreds of heads flinching.

'People of Foulsham,' Moorcus cried. 'People, good people, would you be so foolish as to be taken in by the whining of a child? Do you even know who this girl is? She's a criminal, a thief, she is wanted by the Iremonger police.'

'That's a lie!' I cried.

'She has been about your streets, murdering in the night. She's with the Tailor!'

'Is she? Is she?' went the rumbling populace.

'No I am not,' I cried. 'Don't you believe him, he's just trying to let you drown, stand up to him. Do I look like any tailor? You've seen the posters, all of you have, a tall man, long and stretched. I am just a girl, that's all, a girl of Foulsham. He'd have me murdered, this Iremonger, quick as anything. I'm sixteen years old, I've lived here all my life. My own parents were turned. He knows nothing of what it is to live and die in Foulsham. How many raids have you seen, how many people disappeared in the night? Why won't he let you in? Why won't he let you come through? You've heard the horns, that's what really matters, if the walls come down, you'll drown. He'll watch you! Let us in through these gates, Moorcus Iremonger, or you'll find we're strong enough to break them down. Let us in! Let us in!'

'LET US IN! LET US IN!'

'You will disperse!' Moorcus screamed.

'LET US IN! LET US IN!'

'Oh, please let us in!' an old man wailed.

'You must disperse! You have been warned.'

'Moorcus,' I screamed. 'LET US THROUGH!'

He recognised me then I think, he saw who was with me.

Rowland Cullis saw us too, Rowland was clapping.

'Come again!' yelled Rowland. 'Get him again, smack him.'

'Shut it, Toastrack,' yelled Moorcus, and hit at his birth companion with the butt of his pistol, blood coming quickly, before turning again to face us. 'Clod Iremonger,' his lips seemed to pronounce, though it was so loud about now you could not hear those sounds, but then it was certain he was saying over and again, 'Clod, Clod, Clod.'

He wavered his pistol in our direction, trying to aim it at Clod. He'd shoot I reckoned. Such a look of hate on his face. I tried to push Clod behind me, but in all that struggle at the gates, the sentry had a hold of me through the gate, his hand about my mouth, his arm round my neck, and I could not breathe.

'That's quite enough, little miss,' he said. 'We've had just about enough.'

'Look! Look!' Jenny called. 'Look what they're doing to her!'

Clod was about, quickly enough, and while the sentry had hold of me, he pulled at the sentry's uniform, he ripped it open, brass buttons flying (I thought how Benedict would like them, where was he, where was he now?). Clod's hands scrabbled about, Clod's eyes wide with panic, as he sought to tear the man open, then I had breath again, the sentry staggered back, a hole in him, he stood back.

'Soldiers, help that man!' called Moorcus, and many ran over to him. 'You were warned. And now it is too late. This mob has wounded one of my men. This shall not be tolerated.'

The people of Foulsham were silent then, all mumbling and of a panic. But the soldiers gathered around the sentry stood back now, stood away from him in horror.

'Look! Look!' I tried to call out, but my throat was so hoarse, but they had seen right enough. They had noticed.

The sentry had his hand at his opened gut , which was was leaking sand, it gushed out of him, and he wailed at the sight of it, his mouth wide open but no sound coming out, as sand gushed and gushed from him. And all saw.

'Not real! Not real!'

'What was that?'

'He's made of sand.'

'A man can't be made of sand.'

'Not a man, that wasn't a man.'

'If not a man then what?'

But other soldiers had come then and were now running in formation before the gate and the railings, all with rifles. All at aim.

'People of Foulsham, this is your last chance,' shrieked Moorcus, his voice so high and panicked. 'You must disperse. Go to your homes. Go now and there shall be no further trouble.'

What a sight, all them guns pointing at us. They wouldn't would they, shoot a fellow? Oh they would, they'd gun us all down. We meant as nothing to them. They'd kill us, kill us at the gate. They'd murder in plain sight, in cold blood.

'Aim!' called Moorcus.

At least twenty of the guns aimed particularly at us, at the gate. Oh, Clod, oh Clod, it was a small stand, ours was, it didn't amount to much. People were screaming down the hill, but others were shouting at the soldiers, screaming at them, and the sky was turning black.

Black?

Black already?

A boom then, a great explosion.

That's when I saw, that's when I understood the new screaming. We'd all been looking at the soldiers in front of Bayleaf, or over towards the Heap Wall waiting for it to tumble. We'd none of us been looking towards London, in the other direction, none of us had, but now we could see it.

The blackness. The blackness. It wasn't night. It wasn't night at all, it was fire. Fire! Foulsham was on fire. Whole streets of it must have gone up by then, great gusts of black smoke, not from the chimneys of Bayleaf but from the fire spreading all around us.

'Let us in, oh let us in!' people cried.

'We shall be burnt, burnt to death!'

'Help us! Oh help!'

The soldiers weren't aiming any longer, their guns were pointing down now. They were all staring at the great flames.

Half of Foulsham must be gone, and in such speed. Buildings were falling. People were dying now, the heat was spreading up the hill, smoke was coming and suddenly the rats were with us.

Rats!

Rats everywhere!

Rats, thick about our heels, rats screaming and screeching. They were through the gates in a moment, all screaming, such a carpet of them, whole black fields.

'Get inside!' cried Moorcus to his soldiers. 'Run for cover!'

They went, all those uniformed Iremongers all sprinting inwards, some tripping over the rats, falling to the ground and the rats pouring over them. What a thing, what a thing to be drowned in rat, a hand rising briefly among the horrible moving ground, but then back down again. But the gates, the hot gates, had not been unlocked.

They pushed then the people did, they pushed and crushed and heaved against the railings, threw themselves at them, and all behind likewise, pushing for all their worth as the flames climbed higher from Foulsham. How many people were trampled to death that horror evening, the pushing and coughing, the smoke, the darkness, we shall be trampled on, we shall go under. People climbed over people in their panic, regardless of what was beneath them and what harm it did, the flames coming closer encouraged them so.

But that was what gave me the idea, that was what did it, I shoved Clod up then. I was stronger than him. I heaved him high, shunted him up aside the railings. He was screaming at me, no doubt it was not anything pleasant that he was screaming, but I pushed him up, till my hands were on his heels and then his feet and then I shoved him up again and he was at the spikes by then, so I shoved further, and, I admit it, I climbed on someone myself to get him over. How he shook and screamed but so did so many others. Why should his panic be paid any heed?

Up and up, I had his feet in my hands, pushing him over, couldn't see him any more. There were so many shoving hard against me that I could see nothing for the squashing of all Foulsham people. Up up and then, then, then his feet weren't in my hands any longer. I wasn't holding anything any more. I wasn't with Clod any longer. He'd gone tumbling over, he'd gone, he'd quite gone and I'd lost him all over again. I couldn't move for all the people, smashing against me. Did he make it over, wherever was he?

Go on, Clod man, go on. It hurts to see you go. I hate to see you go.

I'll catch you up, you go ahead, my own dear man. This gate cannot hold forever now, can it? That's logic that is, sure to give.

How the breath was squeezed out of me, shoved out of me.

I thought they'd have me through these bars in pieces the rate they were going, for it really did seem the bars were so up to me that they were actually in me. I tried to cover my face over, I hunched, braced myself as much as ever I could, I closed my eyes and waited for it to happen.

And there she was.

She'd been waiting.

The matchstick woman, the me-me-me thing.

23

BEYOND THE GATES

Clod Iremonger's narrative continued

Within the grounds

I couldn't see her. I couldn't see her at all. There was such a crowding, so many hundreds of people, all the people of Foulsham up against the gates, and the gates leaning in places against the weight of so many, but not giving over. Oh, the people, the trapped people. Where was Lucy? I couldn't see her in all that great thronging.

Just me in so much space, on the path up to Bayleaf House, and behind me such a crushing-crowding, such breathlessness, and the noise, the awful noise behind me, noise of objects calling out from inside so many hundreds of people, how should I ever hear a clay button calling in such confusion? I had to get on, I must get on. I'd stop them. I should stop them, such cries behind me. If only a key, if only there was a key to the gates.

People get lost in wars, trampled over, I see that, there's no individuals only masses, masses being crushed. But I should do it, stop it all. I had the strength for it then. I'd end this horror, maybe. I'd call on all the things that had voice, they'd come to me, I'd command them.

Everything I love I leave behind me this day, the other side of that horror gate, and I shall tumble in, and I mean to do what I can. Behind me the gate was coming down, was leaning over, and more and more people climbing on, other people adding more weight to it, until it bowed ever more, they'd come through, they'd be through in a minute. Quick, Clod, quick, my deafness, before they crush you in their terror and you never find Grandfather.

'Lucy!' I cried, stuck there in the middle.

I turned back a moment, towards the gate, and as I did a seagull swooped down, it flew right at me. It clawed at my hair but I ran on towards the gate. The gull swerved round and came in again, clawing at me, snapping with its beak, screaming at me as if I'd done it some personal wrong. No matter the seagull, it may scream for all it likes. It may snap at me, and bleed me, let it, I'd had worse. I could not see her anywhere, where was she? Quick. Clod, quick, I told myself, get inside or you may never have your chance.

'I am sorry, Lucy. I am sorry. I can think of no other way!'

One last look back, if only I could see her, I should never hope to see her again after. One last look. The railings of Bayleaf House were bending so, they should not hold, all those hands reaching out through them, such screams, and such blackness too and terrible soot, a screen of black darkness, black and thick, as I rushed on towards Bayleaf House, I could barely see it then for all the smoking.

The gull was screaming, screaming. Must get away from it.

The doors were open. The soldiers must have left them like that in their hurrying or couldn't close them for all the rats. Well then, in, in I went, into it, into the cruel lanes of Bayleaf House along all those pipes and pipes and pipes of it, on to find Grandfather, on to an end.

I'm wearing grey flannel trousers. What a man, Clod Iremonger; you're quite coming into yourself. I've aged this day. God keep her, little heart, who knows what shall happen. Who is there that ever knows?

Deaf, so deaf, I couldn't hear anything but bounded on, some bleeding in my ears, all swollen and numbed, poor things, the sounding in my head like a bell, so loud and plain and on a constant shrill note that it was as if all sounds had been removed from the world, as if there was but one sound so complete and plain that it had drowned all others out. But it began ring-ing-ing again, the further I was away from Foulsham people the more the note broke up, and with that shift came more pain as sound began to return, so that I could distinguish distant voices, so many voices, so many names, calling out in agony. As if each was trying to be heard by me, calling, begging, pleading to be heard.

Doors all opened, things all spilled out on the floor, the whole place had been turned inside out, panic was here in these rooms, panic everywhere, panic up and down the House, panic had been there but panic seemed to have fled, for there was no one about, no one at all.

'Halloo!' I cried. 'Hallo! I'm back! 'Tis Clod, Clod himself, who's there that knows me? You sought me I know, well here I am, Clod, I say. 'Tis Clod! Clod! Clod himself!'

That seagull was behind me again, screaming. I ran along, away from it.

I felt there was someone about me, someone very dark, like a shadow creeping along the wall, tickling the surface, yet when I turned there was no one, just empty passageway, and thick black smoke that crawled its way like a dark vein across the ceiling. Yet I felt someone, I was certain that I had. My ears, my ears would know. Give them time, then they'd hear again. They'd separate those names out, then I'd know. Ever less names calling now, ever less.

Where was everyone?

Oh big and abandoned place, where are your people?

There! I walked straight in to them, a great long line of them, hundreds and more, all shuffling out, all in clothing black and dull, old ones and young ones, his and hers, people, people walking through the smoking house, ordinary looking people, not panicked but calm, out into the borough, they had sticks with them and truncheons, they were all headed out, every one of them, and all of their mouths opened just a little and black smoke coming from them and all were not people, they were all guts of dirt, these ones were, souls of sawdust, some of Grandfather's great army, out and out into Foulsham, going in to meet the real people who they imitated, Grandfather's army of defence, into flames and soot. Dummies.

They blocked so much space, Grandfather's army did, they quite choked the corridors, but they were all of a mind, and went out to meet the running hordes who must surely have trampled the gates down. I found a way past them and so down I went down, and down away from them, for there was nowhere else to go but down and down. There was that black smoke again, trailing across the ceiling, it was dripping, I noticed. It dripped tar, the smoke did. It seemed poisonous, somehow very deadly, so down, yes down and down I went to get away from that coiling black smoke that seemed to draw itself along with me, an insubstantial worm, snake more like, growing thicker.

'Grandfather! Grandfather!' I called.

Down, Clod, down and down, calling out for Grandfather, calling for him to come. And then at last there was someone in the distance, further down the curling iron stairway, someone calling back. Someone calling me, calling my name.

My Cousin

I recognised the figure long before I was close. I'd know that figure anywhere, it was part of the heart of me, part of the blood of me, stuff of my bones, was that young man. Back again, come back again to me.

'Tummis! Tummis Iremonger himself!' I cried, for there, down the stairs at the end of a corridor, wandering in confusion, was my tall and my lanky, wearing some long leather coat, there he was with his faint hair that did not persuade and, true to his very form, a seagull flying nearby.

'Oh Tummis, oh my Tummis!' I cried, for I had thought the

dear sweet fellow dead and dead and lost and gone.

'What ho! Clodius, my plug.' I could hear him, my ears were coming back. I could hear him. To hear that voice again that I thought had been silenced forevermore. The sheer wonder of it. 'How do you do these long days of darkness and sooting, and fleeing and flowing, it is ever a pleasure to set eyes on you.'

'Drip! Drip, my drip!' I cried.

'Old plug!'

'Old drip!'

'I got a little lost,' he said. 'I thought I'd gone under in the heaps, did for a bit. It went black for a moment, dirt in my mouth. I tasted that dirt, it was the dirt of death I think, but, in truth, old Clod, old man, old mucker, old joker, old thing of things, I didn't fancy the taste overmuch. I spat it out, and here am I, so to speak, back on dry land, if you'll have it so, if this be solid which I'm not entirely positive, well then here I am, if you see me so, well then I must be me.'

It wasn't a seagull with him, I'd been wrong in that. It was a cat, I saw now, similar colouring to a seagull, but a cat nevertheless. I'd not seen him with a cat before, though he did ever love all animals.

'Come, Clod, my dearest,' he called. He was still a little distance away. 'Come, Clod, ever closer, Clod closer closer Clod, let me hold you. Clod, let me touch you. Clod, come on now. Clod, do come, come up, come here. Clod, come to your old drip. Clod, Clod.'

But that, that was not quite Tummis, was it now, that was not sounding all him, not entirely, not exactly. Something was a little wrong, what was it, what could it be? If I could only hear better. Then I saw it, I saw there was no snot about him, there was no drip from his nose. Perhaps it was just that he'd lost a little of his dripping, that being separated so long from his tap he'd dried up some. And how could he then, I wondered, how could he have survived without his tap, without his Hilary Evelyn? And hadn't you, Clod, hadn't you listened to that old tap on the dreadful night hadn't you heard it, I asked myself. Yes, yes, I certainly had heard it. And what did it say? It said nothing. Dead it was. Dead all over. Oh, come on Clod, don't be cruel, know a friend, know a love when you see one, don't abandon after all that he must have been through.

'Tummis,' I said quietly.

'Here I am!' he said, his arms opened wide, ready to take me in. 'Come, why procrastinate, plunge, plug, in.'

There was a slight panic in his face, but it was not, I think, a Tummis look of panic, and his arms, I thought now, they were not quite the long heron arms of my departed schooldays, they seemed a little shorter to me, and what was that dangling from the end of one? Some sort of huge bat, some great dark thing he'd found fallen from Heap House's attic, but no, that wasn't it, it was an umbrella. Just an umbrella. A plain umbrella. What did he want with that?

'Come here, Clod!' he said. 'Come along. Hurry up, move now, move.'

That didn't sound like Tummis, not at all Tummis that wasn't.

No, Clod. Stop, Clod. I didn't think it was Tummis, not Tummis after all. It was someone else, wasn't it? It was someone trying to be Tummis. But only Tummis could be Tummis. There was only ever one Tummis that I ever knew and that

Tummis, that poor lost never-to-be-forgotten Tummis was a dead Tummis, was *the* dead Tummis, and so this one, this other Tummis, this was a counterfeit. What a thing to do, what new cruelty was this, why would they? How could they? Why fake a Tummis? He must have been waiting for me, he must have been put here just to catch me, and when he'd caught me, what then, what should he do with me?

'Come, Clod! Come on! Here!'

Then I saw I was wrong again, quite wrong, not about Untummis, for certainly it was a very vague Tummis now, Untummis it was for definite. I was wrong about the animal. It wasn't a cat, wasn't after all. I hadn't seen somehow through all that smoke, so much smoke now, thickening the corridor, that black smoke again, that black, black smoke that dripped. Had the fire reached the building then? Was it running inside, up and down corridors, eating its way in and out, growing bigger and braver and blacker and hotter? But that cat, that cat that I thought a cat previously, was a dog now, a great white and grey dog. How had I never noticed that, a great big beautiful thing? What a head it had upon it and what teeth there were to it! How could I have failed to notice such a hound before? Wagging its tail, it was wagging its tail for me. Nice doggy.

'Please come, Clod, old plug, hurry along now, won't you? Don't give up on a chum. Don't throw me over. It's me, *Tummis*!'

Something in the smoky light glinted upon the dog, something small and something metal. I saw it then, all of a sudden, all of a very sudden, suddenly I knew what that was. I had seen it before plain enough. A copper ring it was, I'd known it on a different dark evening. Listen, listen, Clod. I could just hear the copper ring,

'Still am I Agatha Peel, still with her.'

And from the Untummis's arm,

'I am Barnaby Macmillan, oh let me free!'

It wasn't safe, Clod, it wasn't at all safe there. It wasn't right, no, no, it was very wrong. These two, Untummis and his dog, they were wrong, those two, wrong they were, very very wrong. Get out, Clod, get out of there as fast as you may, they'll murder you those two, they mean to unclod Clod.

'Hey!' Untummis called. 'Clod fellow, be a friend to me, won't you?'

I saw something else then, saw it clear, there was a line on Untummis's nose, a growing line, a nose, a glue-on, stuck-on, a made-up moulded nose, a borrowed nose coming off, a pretend Tummis nose, his shape, yes by God it was, his very loving undripping stolen shape, but not his, no-no, never his, they lie these two, they lie and lie and would kill a fellow.

'Why hang back so? Why do you tarry? Plug! My plug!'

The dog's tail was not wagging now, the dog's hackles had gone up, it was growling now, it was barking, but the bark it let out wasn't like any bark I'd ever heard, it was calling out a name, I heard it then, it was shouting-howling a name,

'Unry! Unry!'

'Otta!' called Untummis in a very un-Tummis like voice. 'Otta! Are we seen?'

And then, my Tummis, that vision of my Tummis, fell off, all that was Tummis fell dead and stripped to the floor, like he'd been killed all over again, that thing, that Untummis,

Wrongtummis, Strangetummis, Stolentummis was coming undone, there was a different someone there, someone I'd not known before, a far from Tummis person with holes in his face where his nose should be, and he, this featureless fellow, was screaming.

'Get out! Get out, get away! Get gone!'

And turning and screaming in reply I fled that horror scene. I tried to run along the landing there but a bat flew out, screaming and screeching and so I turned about and went down again, yet further down into the darkness of Bayleaf House.

I was down and down stairs, down deep into the house, and no nearer to Grandfather than when first I entered. There was luggage all about now, so many things packed up and waiting to go, and above me, as if it was following me all through Bayleaf House, that black smoke dancing on the ceiling. Then I saw that there were two figures, beautiful women rising out of the gloom. Tall and lovely women coming out of the fog. I knew them, I knew those ladies well indeed. I'd known them all my life. They weren't real, they were solid through and through, they were marble, always had been. They propped up a great mantel shelf as they always had, but they had moved, they were on a wooden train car, packed up ready to go.

Augusta Ingrid Ernesta Hoffman.

I knew they must come then, other words from another body.

'Clodius,' the voice said, 'are you come?'

And I replied,

'Hullo, Granny.'

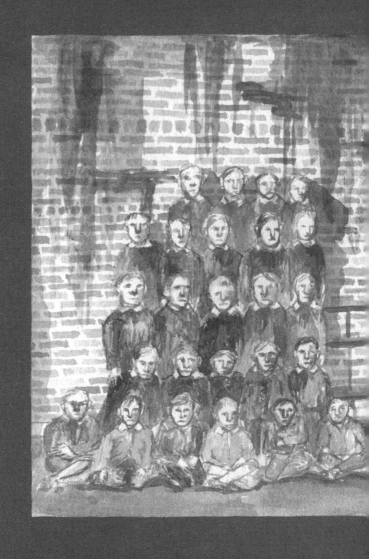

School Children of Foulsham

24

ONWARD FOULSHAM SOLDIERS

Concluding Lucy Pennant's narrative

Jenny had me. Had me by the hair. My red hair, something that stuck out in the black, she pulled and pulled at it. She scrambled all around me and tugged me out. All smashed about, people all around screaming and the smoke and the soot rising from Foulsham, coming up this way. My home, my old home, was burning to bits. What'll there be left of it all after today? Wasn't about winning any more, not about taking them down, was just about survival, was just about staying alive these next minutes, keeping alive, and each minute still breathing in the smoking air well then that was good, that led on to another minute perhaps and if you could grab enough minutes, hold them to you and breathe then, then, then maybe you'd breathe another day.

'She was that close,' I cried, 'that close in to me.'

'What do you mean?'

'We have to go in and I fear it so!'

All the schoolchildren around her, all gathered about, around Jenny and Bug in the thickening smoke.

'We've got to go on in!' I said, coughing out the words. 'All stick together, come on now! Come on in!'

Harder to see anything, ever harder, stumbling along, all that calling out. Chaos really, just chaos everywhere, like the whole world was tilted and broken, like the sun should fall from the sky any minute, that anything that ever had any meaning was gone now, gone forever, that light and life should never come again.

There were calls from everywhere, men and women marching forward in line, other men and women come to meet the first wave of Foulsham people running in, and when they met up with Foulsham people they struck at them, they brought them down.

'Leathers!' I cried. 'They're dummies, don't go near them. Come around with me.'

People being smashed down by those non-people, thumping them down, and no expression on their face, just blankness. We come around through the main office, I think, people calling about, the smoke following in behind us, people coughing all about, and black smoke coming from all those dummies too, black smoke joining the grey smoke from Foulsham, mixing in the air.

On we ran, on and on, thirty of us or so, onward, trying to find better air, we followed the path, followed the pipes into a great hall and all was steam and metal and bangings and callings, and much activity, people rushing about, all in uniform, here was the factory! The factory itself! It was still working, still going on though it was all chaos elsewhere, people, all those people still, people making people. A great buzzing, burning, humming mill. The men running about at their stations, the women in wire cages working on some sort of wheeled machine, metal arms going up and going down, metal wheels running. Things, things being made in the huge Bayleaf House factory. What a place! What a view! Hundreds of workers, a thousand maybe, all in black uniform. Some faces all covered over in leather. Huge warehouse door at one end, must be where all the filth from the heaps were brought in, big enough for a whole ship to be dragged through. What a place it was! What an industry. To see all them small, small people going about making their business. Making things! But what things they were about, what was the purpose behind all this activity, I couldn't rightly say, I could not tell. Bells going off, hammering, shouting, orders barked, a whole world it was. And no one told them to stop, to run for their lives, but on they went. And then I saw at the end were all them pipes clumped together like it was arms of an octopus, there were children there, twenty or so children, and they were being pushed towards the pipes, pushed towards them to breathe life into yet more dummies.

'Children!' I screamed. 'Children there!'

They strapped you down, that's what they did. The end of the pipe with a rubber funnel attached was strapped to your face and then you had no choice but to breathe in, to breathe into them terrible things. And have them suck all out of you.

All of them with me, those kids of Foulsham, oh they saw it all then sure enough. Everything they had hoped for, everything they had dreamed for, this was it, this cruelty was all there ever was. This was what happened when you were ticketed and what had happened to all their friends, and they needed little enough encouragement but we all screamed to a person and pulled and tugged and tried to get them straps off them, to free the poor things before they were all done for.

Leathermen all about, trying to stop us, to smother us with their leather gloves. Anything sharp would do it, glass all over the floor, anything, cut into them dummies and see them leaking out. Smoke coming in there too, filling the factory up.

I struck at one dummy with a fire extinguisher and his head exploded in a black ball of smoke like I'd just kicked a puff ball. You just had to get something sharp into them, pull them open, let all that rubbish out, but with each one cut down there was so much more black smoke coming off them, like they pulled night over everything. But we were at the children then, unstrapping them, tugging them along, and all, all at a scream. Now, now, come along, this air shall suffocate us. They looked to me, they looked to me for help. We were all together in a clump, and what then, and what now? Come on, Lucy, lead them. Lead them, to safety, not to their own deaths. Downwards, ever down. And downwards. Must breathe, musn't we. Down, away from the factory, down to breathe better.

We ran through the corridor of the offices of Bayleaf House, looking for a place to hide, trying handles, hearing running, hearing the pounding of heavy boots beneath us, descending the metal stairs, such a clanking and a screaming, further downwards. Was there anywhere to breathe, any place at all? Clanking, screaming, choking, all choking.

'Come on, come on!' I called, through coughs. 'We're still breathing yet, aren't we? Still breathing, keep at it then, keep coming down!'

Such a noise then, a great tearing, falling, a great blackness, descending, coming on, coming on fast.

An Itch of Iremongers

25

BLOOD

Concluding the narrative of Clod Iremonger

Oh My Family and All Their Things

She was dressed in city clothes, she had on a great hat tied
to her face by a silk scarf lest the wind – or the smoke in this
case – should steal it from her. She had a stick with an ivory
handle, and she looked very strange, very little and very odd to
be out of her room, my grandmother – a turtle without its shell.

'Clodius,' said Granny, 'well, here you are at last. The
eleventh hour, it is true, but you are here at the least, dirty
and bloodied. We should not paint your portrait looking like
that, should we?'

'No, Granny,' I managed barely, 'I don't suppose we should.'

'No indeed, that should never do. An Iremonger covered
in such filth. Come closer, child, son of my Ayris, come to
Granny, kiss me.'

The smoke cleared a little. I saw where I was then. I'd reached the train station of Bayleaf House, and there upon the platform was all of my family. All the servants were there in their uniforms, there was Sturridge the butler, there was Piggott the housekeeper, all clearing in the mist, all those faces at the train station. There were Mr and Mrs Groom the cooks, there was shining Briggs, the underbutler, and all of them, all the servants were bowing to me. Don't do that, I thought, it's very wrong of you to do that, why would you be doing that?

And there was Uncle Aliver, dear doctor, with his curved forceps, bowing and smiling at me, there was Aunt Rosamud with her brass doorhandle, not frowning at me but smiling, so I thought, even sweetly; she's holding Alice Higgs, the poor child, there she is so locked in brass, little little mudlark, gagged child. There was Uncle Timfy, cruel house uncle, his pig-nose whistle at his lips, beside him his twin, the Governor of Birth Objects, grinning widely as always, Uncle Idwid, wicked Uncle Idwid, Geraldine Whitehead held close.

I saw all those others too. I saw dear pale Ormily, holding fast to her watering can. Oh Ormily, I am glad that you did not see what I had just seen, that abhorration of our long and dripping friend. All of them, every cousin of mine, had their birth objects about them in all the upheaval, cleaving it to them, never to part. Of all of them, of all this sudden shock and crowding and great thick fug of my family, of all of them I was not unhappy to see poor, poor Ormily, Tummis's Ormily.

There was my cousin Bornobby too, his shoe birth object slung upon his shoulder, there was Cousin Pool and Cousin Theeby. I think they must have married since I last saw them.

There was Cousin Foy with her great ten-pound weight. So many of them, so many I hadn't thought of in all my dark adventuring. But there was one I saw now, there was one I had, certainly I had thought of, I had seen her in my dreams and they had not been happy, those dreams: there she stood, Cousin Pinalippy, my once betrothed. I could not imagine she could be betrothed to me any longer, not after all that had happened. Surely I had shunned off that dark lip for good and all, surely I'd never have to doily no more. But she waved at me a little. It seemed to me those unsought-for lips may even be blowing me some sort of a mangled kiss.

My family shouldn't do all this. They shouldn't. They shouldn't just be standing there. Why were they all looking at me, smiling, nodding and bowing so? They should run at me, trample me down, but they didn't and then there was a sudden smacking sound. In a terror I wondered if a gun had gone off, if I'd been shot, if there was blood dripping out of me, I shouldn't have been surprised of that, not in the least, but then the smacking sound continued and I saw what it came from. My family, the servants, they were clapping, every one of them, their claps resounding upon the ceiling, echoing down the long smoking chamber of the tunnel.

Wrong! Quite wrong to do that.

My turn to move my head at them, not to nod, to shake it, to shake.

'Stop! Stop!' I said. 'You must not do that. I hate that you do that.'

'Come, come,' said Granny, 'kiss me.'

I had never been able to disobey Granny, never in my life. I

311

felt myself tumbling, falling headlong back into my childhood, a place I would far rather not revisit. I stepped forward a little. I could not do otherwise. I leant forward and kissed the cobweb cheek of Granny and felt indeed that I was in a web trapped then, that the grey grey hairs of my grandmother, the mothlike, flylike, spiderlike hairs, were winding all around me and quite tying me up in horrible knots of family and love and bribery and guilt, such knots that might drown a soul.

'Oh, what's to be done?' I whispered.

'Good child,' she said, 'you are an Iremonger. You shall always be, Clodius, an Iremonger, you know.'

'I suppose I will, Granny, though I think I am not much good at it.'

'Nonsense! Stand straight! Breathe in! There now. Chest out! Better, better. You have done us great service, Clodius, you have been most useful. We never could have got the Tailor without your help, and we should never otherwise have had Rippit, restored to us.'

'No!' I cried. 'No, I never . . .'

'Yes, yes, Clod, yes you did. That was very well done, very properly done indeed. Prettily done. We knew you should, otherwise we should never have let you out of our ever-loving and protecting arms, but we must let you go on your little wandering. We gave some length to your lead, and then when we declared it was time, and not a moment before, we gave that lead of yours, that invisible strong thread, we gave it a good tug, like plucking on your aorta, Clodius, pinching at the vessels that surround your own weak heart, and you came back, and here you are, a true Iremonger always comes back.

Ayris's son should always come back. There's something of her there in your face. Ayris, Ayris my darling girl. This little you left us, Ayris. This brave shambling form.'

'Granny. I think, Granny – no, I know, Granny – I am a bad Iremonger, the very worst. I think, Granny, all in all, I should be thrown out. Granny, I must be going now.'

'Going, going, must you?'

'Yes, indeed. Goodbye all, I am right glad to have seen you. But I cannot stay, I am not worthy –'

'Where, Clod, where is it that you are going?'

'Back up there,' I said. 'Foulsham.'

Some laughter, small thin laughter, from my family thereabouts.

'There is no Foulsham, Clod, not any more. Foulsham is done with.'

'How can you say that, Granny, all those people up there?'

'Heap House has fallen, Clod,' she said. 'It has quite come down. My room, room of my life, has fallen, it lies in the dust. We didn't do it, it was them, it was London's bidding. London has murdered Foulsham. And London shall repent it.'

'All gone! All gone!' I cried. 'Has it truly? But, but all those people, they must be helped, some can yet be saved. My Lucy is up there!'

'Typical of the child, no pluck, no spirit. Stand up, Clod, be upright, grow tall: understand and act upon it. We have been waiting for you and now we must on.'

'Waiting,' I stammered, 'waiting for me?'

'We knew you should come. You took your time, true enough, how like you that is. Never mind, you are here now, as we

313

knew you should be. Everything in its place.'

'Granny, I did not know I should be here, indeed I did not.'

'That's of little importance.'

'I find I don't want to be here. I don't want to be here at all.'

'Don't be weak, Clod, don't be wet. We shall have no wetness. You've been herded here, Clod, moved along, encouraged to us. Pushed at corners, dragged in places, until you came upon us. We gather our own up, every one of us, without fail. We have even gathered our lost child Binadit, and that indeed was unexpected. Rosamud's bastard son, who she lost out in the heaps so long ago after her own Milcrumb was drowned there. Come back now, hasn't he, Rosamud, your own guilt.'

'Yes, dear Ommaball, he has come to his mummy at last.'

'And we keep him on his own, all alone in an empty lead-lined carriage, where nothing might find him out.'

'Do you mean Benedict, do you mean Benedict Tipp?'

'I mean Binadit Iremonger, lovechild, the bastard. We'll take him, we acknowledge him, we'll collect him up. So then, we are all complete.'

'He'll bring the heaps down.'

'Very like, Clod. And so there's nowhere else to go, is there then, dear boy, crumb of my lost lovely, only down that tunnel in the other direction.'

'Into London?'

'Yes, London. There to lay our traps, there to put down our poison, there to rise again another day. The tunnel's been dug right through, right under them, into London. We'll break our vow. Iremongers shall on London tread!'

'But . . . but a tunnel, how?'

'Umbitt's men, they did it. Umbitt's clever fools!'

'My men,' came a deep voice, 'my dirty army.'

'Grandfather!'

And there along the platform, one figure moving against the direction of the crowd. Great long figure. Huge figure. Old and gloom itself. My grandfather. Now I might! Now! Now!

'Jack Pike. Jack Pike.'

'I call you all,' I said, 'I call you all, Percy Hotchkiss, Little Lil, Mr Gurney, Albert Powling, Alice Higgs, come now John Julius Middleton, Muriel Binton come, come Perdita Braithwaite, even come Geraldine Whitehead, strike, strike now. Strike fast!'

Nothing.

Nothing moved.

Ormily's can twitched once in her hand.

'I command you, Lieutenant Simpson, Annabel Carrew, come Amy Aiken, come Mark Seedly, come Gloria Emma Utting. Come up, I command it!'

The watering can, the shoe, the weight, even, wheeled up in the air, twisting, turning towards Grandfather. And Grandfather, seeing all this traffic coming towards him, waved his hand at them like they were no more than flies, and all tumbled down again, their flight so short.

'Grandfather, sir,' I screamed, 'I mean to kill you!'

'Do you, Clod?'

'He's our blood, Umbitt. Remember. He's Ayris's child,' said Granny.

'I will kill you, Grandfather!'

'Ayris is dead, Ommaball. She's never coming back.'

'Clodius, you are an Iremonger. You know you are.'

315

'Please, my lady,' said housekeeper Piggott, coming forward. 'My lady, there is not much time. The fire, my lady, the fire arrives!'

Indeed the smoke was coming back now and everyone's face was dripping with sweat.

'And here,' said Grandfather, 'is Rippit restored to us.'

Such a strange shrunken, flattened figure stood out from behind Grandfather. Like someone had been playing with his bones, melting them down, but only reached halfway through the procedure before being disturbed. In his hands he had a long, rusted knife. I knew it to be Alexander Erkmann before ever I heard the Tailor's weak voice.

'Rippit,' said cousin Rippit.

'Yes, Rippit, here you are among us.'

'Rippit,' he said.

'Hello, cousin,' I ventured weakly, 'there you are again.'

'Rippit,' he said.

'Is that all he says?' I asked.

'Rippit,' said Rippit.

'It is for now,' said Grandmother. 'In time we shall recover him. And we have thought it best, since you have had such an adventure together, that Rippit should be your companion, that Rippit should look after you.'

'Rippit,' said Grandfather, a great misery on his face. 'Rippit shall Iremonger you, Rippit shall bring you back into shape.'

Then shrunken Rippit pulled at his pocket. I recognised the dirty cloth with which the Tailor had wrapped him when he was but a hip flask. From under that cloth came a new noise:

'James Henry!' I cried. 'You have James Henry!'

'Yes, yes, child, your plug,' said Grandfather. 'Rippit shall hold him for you, for a while. Until you earn him back.'

'Excuse me, my lady,' said Butler Sturridge. 'I am sorry to mention it, but unless we are very soon underway, I fear it may be too late.'

'James Henry Hayward! James Henry Hayward!'

Oh please, oh please do not cry out so, oh my plug.

'Clodius,' said Granny, 'be an Iremonger! Clodius, you will be an Iremonger, you will earn those trousers!'

'Oh, Granny,' I cried, 'I am that broken.'

Some planking, some brick fell from the ceiling onto the platform, setting some of my family screaming. A clattering of footsteps, in rushed hateful Unry with Otta clumping beside him.

'The house is going!' he cried. 'The railings have gone down, the whole house is swarming with Foulsham people, all in a terror, they're coming down, they're coming, the building, the building, it won't hold! It cannot hold!'

'Come, come now, all my gathering blood,' said Grandfather, 'step in, we leave this place, we shall break the curse.'

'I quite need a holiday,' said Granny.

My family and the servants rushed, pushing and shunting, into the waiting carriages.

'Get on the train, get on the train!' cried Sturridge.

'I may stay, I think,' I managed.

'You shall not, indeed,' said Granny.

Moorcus was behind me, with several of his officer men, and I was picked up and bundled in like any twist of paper.

'Lucy, Lucy!' I cried.

317

'Please Clodius!' said Granny. 'Will you think! You'll upset Pinalippy. We shall have you married, and soon. There now, there's something to look forward to: a fixture!'

I was pushed down into a seat, squashed Rippit beside me, staring bitterly at me through his ruddy eyes. I lurched for the window but was pushed back down.

'Lucy! Lucy!'

'I see you are going to be tiresome,' said Granny.

'LUCY!'

'She's dead, Clod, she's gone,' said Granny, a very horrible look on her face.

There was a terrible tumbling, cracking, smashing. There was the most enormous crashing, like the whole world had tripped over, like we were buried deep now in our graves.

'The Heap Wall, the Heap Wall is down then,' said Granny, with no more seriousness than if she'd lost a button from her jacket. 'Foulsham is over.'

'Oh Foulsham's gone! It's gone! Lucy, oh Lucy,' I cried. 'LUCY!'

The train screamed as if answering me and we lurched forwards, into London.

Miss Eleanor Cranwell

26

OBSERVATIONS FROM A NURSERY

Beginning the narrative of Eleanor Cranwell, 23 Connaught Place, London W

I mean to write it all down, just as Mr Pepys did before me. He saw the Great Fire of London and from the look of the flames in the distance maybe I shall witness something similar. I've been sat at the window since the first explosion went off. Nanny's been in several times to tell me I must sleep now. She says it's nothing to worry about, that all the flames shall long be put out before they come anywhere near Connaught Place. It is true that there has been little enough adventure on our street, nothing more of interest than the house opposite, where the Carringtons live, having a case of the cholera, poor souls, and now their house is all shut up over there and no one comes in or out. Even so, I keep at my post, my diary in my lap.

The wind's got up terribly. I sit at my window still. There's everything blowing down the street, how the wind does rattle all about. Our house itself seems to move as if it has the shivers, I hope it's not going to catch the ague, our own dear house. I wonder whether this wind will put the flames out or blow them over here.

There's some people on the street now. I don't think I've seen anyone like that. A whole load of them it looks like, a whole family all dressed up like they've been on a trip. I wonder who they are. There're servants with them too, a great deal of servants, and men in lines coming after. They're going to the house opposite. They can't go in there, there's illness there, it isn't safe. Someone should tell them, the whole house has been quarantined.

Ah, but someone is coming to tell them, it's one of the servants from next door, she's running up to the people on the street. She's being pointed to the old man in the tall top hat, she goes up to him, does a quick bow. The old man looks round at her, there's an old woman beside him, most peculiarly dressed. I wonder whoever they are, there's a strange look to them, I feel, like they do not know how to dress, as if they'd been given a manual about it, only they had not read it over correctly. I wonder what they're doing here.

The servant's talking to the old man, she's explaining it all. I am so glad of it, because it's been made very clear to us all that we're not to go near that house, not for any reason. The old man doesn't seem to like being disturbed, he has such a frown on his face. He turns and grimaces now, raises a gloved hand and gestures impatiently at the servant, his fingers move as if he were flicking water at her.

I cannot explain what I saw next, only that I am certain that I did see it.

No matter how impossible it is.

I must try to put it down properly.

The poor servant from 32!

Here I go, then.

A moment after the old man flicked his finger at her, she fell down the steps, it was a strange falling, not like anything I have ever seen before, she seemed to spin around and around, to shrink and shrivel, and tumble so. She fell to the ground, quite to the ground. Only, I swear this is the truth, only when she was upon the ground, the moment she hit it, she was no longer a servant at all. She was a music stand. A music stand. She wasn't a servant at all. I swear I saw it. And one of the other people of the party, a young man – quite handsome – in a strange policeman's uniform, with a brass helmet and some sort of medal upon his chest, he kicked the music stand out of the way, further along the street.

I know I saw that.

I do swear that I did.

My hands have been shaking so much. I'm trying very much to keep calm and sensible. To be sensible, that is the thing. The strange family have moved in opposite, they've all gone in there now. There was such a group of them. They shall fill it very easily. Whatever has become of the Carringtons that used to live there before?

Among the family I saw going in were: the old man and the old woman; the fellow in the helmet; a small blind man and with him a similarly small man who kept a whistle to his lips, a tough-looking lady with a brass doorhandle, a haughty-looking lady, about my age, her head held high and beside her a kinder, fair-haired girl holding of all things a watering can. There were many others that followed, going forwards in a line, being ticked off a list by the handsome man in the helmet. Towards the end I saw an even more shrunken fellow, about half the height of all the others, and beside him, rather uncomfortably, I thought, a young man with a prominent forehead and very black hair in a parting, he turned around, he did. Great black circles under his eyes, or smudged as if he had been crying, his suit was very messy, unlike the others.

Who were these people? What ever was going on? He seemed to know I was looking, that unkempt young man. He turned to me, looked right up at the window, he seemed to see me for an instant. I thought he tried to smile at me, but the tiny man beside him took a tug to his arm and he went inside then with all the others. Last of all several men came in odd leather garments, between them an enormous figure, some sort of giant.

They have entered now, the entire family, under cover of night. I shouldn't have seen them but for the gas streetlighting. There's something very wrong about them, something that should not be allowed.

It is morning at last. It was all a dream, surely, a strange dream. I am subject to fancy dreams. Nanny tells me that I'm not to read so many books, that if I continue at my current rate I shall read myself quite to death. Well then, she must be right. Somehow I must have slept at my window post and had the strangest dream. It is morning now, the house opposite is as shut as ever it was, and I'm sure the poor Carringtons are convalescing inside. A strange dream indeed. But it was so vivid. I cannot shake it from my mind.

I called on Martha, the tweeny maid, to do a favour for me. She said of course she should, anything to bring the colour back to my cheeks. I told her to go out into the street and see if she could find a bent music stand there. She looked puzzled, but obliged. I'm sure she shall not find any such object and then all shall be forgotten, then I shall be able to sleep quite peacefully.

Martha's just come and gone away again.

I have the music stand in my hands.

It is strangely warm.

It was not a dream then, not a dream at all.

Acknowledgements

I would like to thank the really amazing team at Hot Key for all their help and support with this trilogy: Sarah Odedina, Jenny Jacoby, Kate Manning, Sarah Benton, Megan Farr, Jet Purdie, Cait Davies, Sanne Vliegenthart, Naomi Colthurst and Livs Mead. Sara O'Connor, wonderful editor, remains the Iremongers' best friend in the world and Jan Bielecki has been brilliant and possesses a patience greater than Job's. I would also like to thank Hadley Dyer, Tracy Carns, Elisabetta Sgarbi and Pierre Demarty for letting the Iremongers come to their countries.

Everyone at Blake Friedman has been enormously industrious with these books, I must acknowledge all the work and care of Tom Witcomb and Louise Brice, and most of all, and as always, my wonderful agent Isobel Dixon, without whom I'd come undone, completely.

Edward Carey

Edward Carey is a playwright, novelist and illustrator. He has worked for the theatre in London, Lithuania and Romania and with a shadow puppet master in Malaysia. He has written two illustrated novels for adults — OBSERVATORY MANSIONS and ALVA AND IRVA — both have been translated into many different languages. He lives in Austin, Texas, where he wrote the Iremonger Trilogy because he missed London and rain. Follow Edward on Twitter: @EdwardCarey70 or find out more about his books at edwardcareyauthor.com.

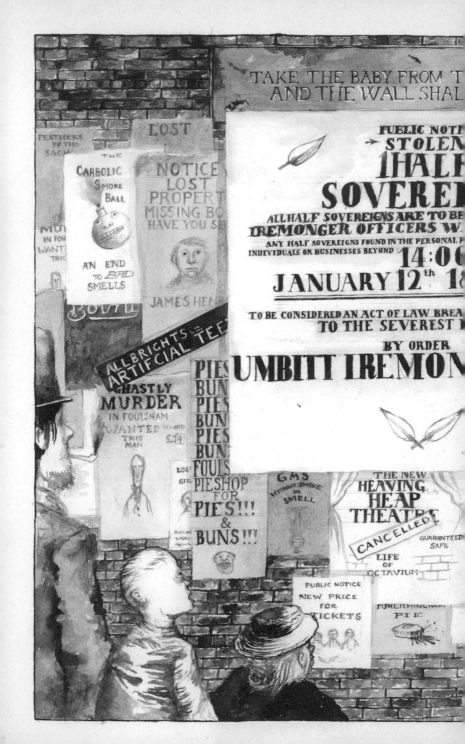